AND THEN YOU DIE

By

James H Longmore

A HellBound Books Publishing LLC Book
Austin TX

James H Longmore

A HellBound Books LLC Publication

Copyright © 2021 by HellBound Books Publishing LLC
All Rights Reserved

Cover and art design by Kevin Enhart for
HellBound Books Publishing LLC

Edition 2

No part of this book may be reproduced, stored in a retrieval system, or transmitted by any means, electronic, mechanical, photocopying, recording or otherwise without written permission from the author
This book is a work of fiction. Names, characters, places and incidents are entirely fictitious or are used fictitiously and any resemblance to actual persons, living or dead, events or locales is purely coincidental.

www.hellboundbookspublishing.com

Printed in the United States of America

BY JAMES H LONGMORE

HORROR
Blood & Kisses
'Pede
Tenebrion
Flanagan

BIZARRO
The Erotic Odyssey of Colton Forshay
Buds
And Then You Die
Feeder
I Am Joe's Unwanted Penis

James H Longmore

AND THEN YOU DIE

James H Longmore

ONE

Claire Jepson eased her foot down on the gas pedal and gripped the steering wheel with one hand. She watched as the Aston Martin's speedometer crept closer to eighty, and she rubbed at the dull ache in her grumbling belly with her other hand.

She caught a quick glimpse of her face in the rear-view. To her horror, Claire saw her usually pretty features looked pale and miserable and were coated with a feverish sheen of sweat that made her look far, far older than her thirty-seven years. It was upsetting because Claire had always taken pride in her appearance and had worked hard at keeping her petite body trim and firm. Not an easy task in her whirlwind world of seemingly endless business lunches.

She'd had her own gym equipment installed at the office, so she could simultaneously work out *and* work; she refused to use the gym she had so generously provided for her staff because she preferred to sweat and grunt in private. Plus, working out had a tendency to give Claire a raging wide-on, and she'd invariably end each session with one hand down her sweaty yoga pants, fingers busy jilling herself to a gushing, scream-out-loud orgasm.

The stabbing pains in Claire's belly were making her regret the decision she'd made to drive to and from the business conference instead of flying. Whilst she relished the enforced solitude of a long road trip, right now she could kill for a gin and tonic and the comfort of a close-by, cramped restroom.

Keeping a nervous eye on the road ahead, Claire kept a look out for the ominous, telltale white snouts of the cop cars that secreted themselves down the farm tracks that littered both sides of this stretch of lonely Texas highway. There they'd sit like patient predators waiting to pounce; not usually having to wait too long before some otherwise law-abiding citizen sped by on their way to something important. The inevitability of Murphy's Law dictated that Claire would be pulled this morning, and that was certainly the very last thing she needed right now.

Claire's stomach lurched once again, and an uncomfortable heat settled in her lower intestine. She stepped on the gas pedal some more and prayed that she hadn't missed the rest stop.

To add to her misery, Claire was also experiencing feelings of guilt. This was an emotion alien to her, and it chuntered away at the back of her mind like a restless spirit.

Last night she'd been unfaithful to Karl.

She hadn't planned for it to happen, and it was certainly not the kind of behavior that Claire would have ever expected from herself. The whole sorry incident had been just an unfortunate set of circumstances.

Claire had been flattered to receive the invitation to be the keynote speaker at the National Software Business Symposium in New Orleans. They'd selected the inspirational Claire Jepson as one of the few successful dot com entrepreneurs whose name wasn't Zuckerberg or Omidyar; or who didn't have a penis.

She'd delivered an incredibly uplifting and insightful speech to the rapturous applause from her peers, and then she'd bumped into some random guy in the conference center bar. He'd seemed nice, charming even, but the most remarkable thing that Claire could remember about him was just how *ordinary* he was. In retrospect, it was the man's ordinary-ness that had seemed the most extraordinary thing about him.

They'd shared a drink or three, and Claire had found herself incredibly flattered at the attention she was getting from the sexy, younger man—Claire figured him for mid-twenties—what with her approaching forty and her biological clock ticking so fucking loud she was sure he would be able to hear it. Claire struggled to remember the last time she'd been on the receiving end of such interest; certainly not in the two years she'd been with Karl.

So, when the guy had invited Claire to join him for a meal at a cozy little Indian restaurant he knew, Claire hadn't declined.

The fun of it was that Claire didn't even like Indian food, or more to the point, Indian food didn't like her. She had always found it much too spicy, and it played havoc with her guts. This, Hypochondriac Claire was convinced were the early signs of IBS. But Claire couldn't stand the thought of another night in a characterless hotel room, eating room service boot-leather steak and attempting to get off to pay-per-view porn that never seemed to cater to the female clientele.

After dinner, which was accompanied with a seemingly endless procession of Tiger beer, Claire's mystery man had whisked her off to some dingy underground nightclub. The rest of the night had been an alcohol-hazed whirl of pounding trance music, which mixed in her mind with the jazzy resonance of some long-forgotten, favorite song, crazy arm-flailing dancing and of slurping tequila off a barman's rock-hard, sweat-salted abs. Then there had come the inevitable finale to Claire's nighttime odyssey; back to her hotel suite with her new friend—damned if she could remember the guy's name, or if she'd even asked for it—for rough, urgent sex that was so animalistic that Claire couldn't remember if they'd used protection or not.

What she *could* remember, however, was that her beau had taken her in the ass, which was particularly memorable because it was something Karl had always refused to do, no matter how much she begged. Claire had found that strange about her fiancé because she'd thought that *all* men craved a little back door action from time to time; along with many women.

Claire's sexual leanings had always been towards the scatological. She had been just eleven when her drunken father had woken her up in the middle of the night by peeing on her. In his defense, he'd been so out of his head with single malt that he had genuinely mistaken his daughter's bed for the lavatory.

Thus, the seeds were sown.

As Claire matured, she'd sought out boyfriends who would pee on her - and upon whom she could pee - and from there she quickly graduated to full-on scat play. She'd lost count of the number of guys and girls she'd scared off by asking them to crap on her tits. And there was one guy, Simon Something-or-other, who'd freaked completely out when she'd fished one of his turds from the toilet, frozen it solid and used it as a dildo.

...and Then You Die

Truth was, Claire enjoyed the fetish so much that she'd lost her anal cherry to Ethan Foote—one of the meatheads on the high school football team—a full two years before she'd let him into her cunt.

So, when her mystery one-night stand had slipped his cock with ease inside her ass from behind, Claire had said nothing. In fact, he'd gotten her so goddamned wet with his mouth and fingers that her pussy juice had bubbled out and dribbled down to lube up her puckered, brown rose, a treat. She'd relaxed herself to accommodate his not inconsiderable cock and then reached down to insert two fingers into her vagina. Then, in a little signature move she liked to call *shaking hands*; Claire had massaged his dick from deep inside herself.

She'd awoken the next morning with her head still spinning and the early onset of the inevitable hangover from hell. Her mystery one-night stand was gone, and Claire's first instinct had been to fear the worse and assume she'd been robbed; it is a wealthy woman's burden to entertain the assumption that it is always her money that people find the most attractive.

Claire had forced herself out of bed—throbbing head and all—and checked through her stuff. Nope, everything was still there: wallet, cash, credit cards, the five-thousand dollar watch that had been a gift from Karl on the event of their first anniversary as a couple (paid for with her own hard-earned, of course, but still a lovely gesture). In fact, as Claire had examined the hotel room, it had looked to all intents and purposes as if her casual pick-up had never been there at all. If it weren't for the exquisite ache deep in her ass, Claire could have easily convinced herself—and her conscience—that she'd dreamt the whole sordid tryst.

A resonant rumble in her belly served Claire a

warning that the rest stop was not coming up anywhere near fast enough. She dared a little more pressure on the gas pedal and watched the speedometer needle twitch once more to the right.

Guessing her problem to be trapped gas exacerbated by the long trip, Claire decided that the best thing she could do to afford some temporary relief to her poor, aching guts would be to alleviate some of the pressure. She shifted her weight onto one buttock and eased out a controlled, silent fart.

"Ahhhhh," Claire sighed to herself and felt the immediate relief as her pain subsided. She wrinkled her nose at her own stink and rolled a window down to let it out. She could smell a stomach-churning blend of dopiaza, tequila and semen—and the latter neatly answered her protection (or lack thereof) conundrum.

Dammit! How could she have been so fucking stupid?

Now she'd have to get herself tested without Karl finding out, and Claire knew for sure that that wasn't going to be a walk in the goddamned park.

And so, Claire drifted into the self-loathing phase of her guilt. How could she have done such a thing to her poor, cuckolded Karl? He was her *person*, her partner for over twenty-four months, her soon to be husband. It wasn't even as if she didn't love the guy; Karl rocked her world and made everything feel right. Hell, she even loved the way they had become *Claire'n'Karl* to their social circle—she loved their cutesy combined name because it sounded as if they were already joined together.

Karl was a simple soul and had always been intimidated by Claire's success. He would often feel inadequate in the shadow of self-made millionaire Claire Jepson and was convinced that he was not attractive enough (which was actually bullshit, Karl was twelve years junior to Claire and had youthful good looks, an incredible, six feet, one-inch, muscular body and a glint in his eye that could seduce anyone). Oh yeah, there was also his constant worry that he was not smart enough for her, which was again, bullcrap; he *was* intelligent enough to harbor aspirations of being a teacher. Sadly, that had all kind of petered out once he'd hopped aboard the Claire Jepson gravy train.

Between the hot pain that wracked her insides and the guilt that was doing a similar job on her conscience, Claire didn't think that she could actually feel much worse about herself right now. She knew in her heart that Karl would most likely forgive her drunken indiscretion and would punish her far less than Claire was essentially punishing herself; had Claire been a *Believer*, she would have thought that the fire currently raging in her lower intestine was her due punishment from God.

Encouraged by the earlier flatus success, Claire shifted her weight once more and dared herself to squeeze out a little more gas.

"Shit!" Claire cried out. She felt her bowels let go a little more than planned and a warm, sticky wetness bubbled into her panties. "Shit, shit, shit!" She thumped a hand on the steering wheel, and she felt even dirtier than she had before.

Claire felt like crying; she could feel the hot mess squelching around between her butt cheeks and beginning to soak through her skirt, and she was grateful that the Aston had leather seats. She also noted, as she raced past a billboard advertising divorce attorneys, that she was—ironically—only a minute away from the grungy motel on the outskirts of town that served as the indicator that Claire was less than fifteen minutes from home.

There it was, looming on the horizon as if to mock

Claire and the sickening mess in her underwear.

RANDYS' ROADSIDE MOTEL
Room's by the hour

"Goddammit," Claire growled and hit the blinker. She pulled into the motel's sparsely populated car park. The pressure was building up inside her once more, but she was too shit scared to dare let any of it out again. It rumbled and swished around like boiling acid, and the pain made her feel quite faint.

Claire slammed on the brake, and her car jerked to a stop in the center of two parking spaces—one of them the disabled—in front of the motel's office. She clambered from the car and raced into the reception area, where she was greeted by an obese, filthy looking individual who she presumed to be Randy.

"Can ah help ya?" Randy drawled as he picked crusty sleep from the corner of his eyes with dirt-blackened fingernails.

"Toilet? Please." Claire grunted through gritted teeth. She continued on towards the restroom, oblivious to the hand-written card stuck to the rear of the cash register with clear tape.

RESTROOM'S ARE FOR CLIENTELE ONLY!!!

"Thank you!" Claire waved a hand over her head at him. She kept the other firmly clasped to her stomach, as if afraid to let go in case her abdominal contents would burst out.

Claire barely made it to the stall just in time. She hiked up her skirt, kicked off her soiled panties and sat down heavily on the cold plastic. There was no time even to wipe the dark yellow pee splashes off of the seat. She ground her teeth against the pain, as her bowels opened, and the poop splashed from her in a constant, liquid stream.

As unpleasant as it was, there was no escaping the overwhelming sense of relief Claire felt as her body evacuated the sour mix of spicy food and alcohol. The sickly stench assaulted Claire's nose and made her throat gag. But, at the same time, there was that faintest whiff of jizz that conjured in her mind erotic flashbacks of her previous evening. Heaving, sweating bodies and busy mouths and fingers and that magnificent, hard dick that had pounded away at her ass.

With her mind switched to carnal thoughts, Claire's mind became focused on the exquisite scalding of diarrhea on an anus made sore by vigorous, anonymous sodomy, and she couldn't help but reach a hand down between her legs and seek out her tingling clit.

When she'd finished up, Claire felt a billion times better. In less than five minutes she'd vacated the entire contents of her digestive system and come twice in swift succession.

Claire wiped and flushed and set to the business of dealing with the fallout. She picked her soiled panties up off the pube-strewn floor and stuffed them into one of the feminine hygiene bags that were stacked next to the lavatory. The paper bag had a picture of a demure yet smug looking Victorian lady on it, as if the Victorians had invented menstruation or something.

She did briefly consider dumping the paper bag into the trash but decided against it. Karl would definitely notice the panties missing when she got home, such was the nature of his OCD-driven paranoia. Karl did all of their laundry, and it was he who had bought said undergarments for his lover; they were his favorites, and Claire had worn them especially for her homecoming. Whenever Claire returned from one of her frequent business trips, Karl would discretely sniff her for alien cologne and search through her dirty laundry for unexplained stains (she was half-convinced that was the only reason he *insisted* on doing the damned laundry). And in bed, under the auspices of lovemaking, she would often catch him examining her body for telltale scratches or hickeys.

At least this time, Karl's paranoia wouldn't be unfounded.

Claire washed her hands in the tepid water, dried them on a rough paper towel and exited the restroom with the hygiene bag clutched firmly in her hand.

"I can't thank you enough," she said to Randy, who peered at her, bemused. "That's the last time I eat Indian food." Claire forced a smile.

"S'okay," Randy replied. "Only them's restrooms is only for payin' customers."

"I understand." Claire made eye contact with the man, mostly to avoid herself gawking at the improbably fat belly that made him appear eight months pregnant. "How much do I owe you?"

Randy cracked a grin at her that wrinkled his weather-beaten face and showed off his badly capped teeth.

"Jus' put in a donation to ma' charity here, and we'll call it square." Randy pointed to a collection tin perched on the reception desk. The tin declared that the collection was for the *Spastics,* and Claire wasn't so sure that you were supposed to call them that anymore and so was dubious as to the age—and validity—of said tin.

Still, Claire was more than grateful for the relief that Randy had inadvertently allowed her, and she slipped a couple of Ben Franklins into the slot at the top of the tin.

"Why, thank ya, Ma'am." Randy beamed and pulled

up his breeches. "You're a saint."

"No. Thank *you*, Randy." Claire smiled back. She thought of the poor old sap cleaning up the reeking, spattered mess she'd just left behind on the sides of the toilet bowl, and she began to wonder if two hundred was enough. Claire toyed with the idea of suggesting to Randy that he leave it ten minutes before venturing into the restroom but decided in the end that that would be just a little too crass.

"Don't mention it, Ma'am." Randy grinned. "Have yersel' a nice day." Claire stepped out into the fresh, morning sunshine and sighed the biggest of sighs. The warmth of the sun on her face, along with a wonderfully empty belly and finally receding hangover, made Claire feel marginally better about facing Karl. She gripped the hygiene bag tight by its top and made her way back to the car.

The sound of voices caught Claire's attention. She turned around and squinted across the weed-strewn courtyard. There, she saw a young couple on their way to one of the motel rooms. They giggled and pawed at each other like a pair of love-struck teenagers heading under the bleachers. The girl unlocked the door and stumbled backwards into the room, yanking the guy inside by his arm. More giggles, and then the door slammed shut.

Karl?

No, it couldn't possibly be.

Claire shook her head as if to clear the silly notion from her fogged brain, and she admonished herself for being foolish. But in that split second of seeing the guy with the short-haired brunette, Claire was positive that it *was* her Karl.

"You're still drunk, Claire-baby," she told herself. But, then again, the young guy sure had looked a lot like her fiancé.

Claire felt her stomach churn in a familiar sensation. She *felt* that there was something wrong, and she knew well enough to trust her gut feeling. As much as she wanted to run and hide and pretend that she hadn't just seen what she knew she had seen, Claire Jepson had never been one for not rooting out the truth.

As she contemplated her next move, Claire considered just how ridiculous she must look in her Chanel skirt suit—with accompanying silk shirt—two-thousand-dollar shoes, symposium name badge dangling by a blue nylon lanyard around her neck and clutching a sanitary pad disposal bag stuffed with soiled underwear. The thought gave her a short-lived smile.

She strode with purpose towards room 26, the one the guy-who-looked-like-Karl-but-who-couldn't-possibly-be-Karl had been willingly dragged into.

Claire paused by the grimy, cracked window. The room's occupants had not even bothered to close the curtains as they were all too wrapped up in each other—or quite possibly were overt exhibitionists. She screwed up her eyes, not really wanting to look, but knowing that she really had no choice. Claire told herself that this was simply her mind playing mean tricks on her as fair punishment for her own indiscretion the night before. It still took every grain of the substance that was Claire Jepson to do what she had to do.

In any other circumstance, she would have been proud of her own resolve.

A deep breath and Claire peeped through the motel room window. Although the ragged, bug-strewn spider webs and the dirty glass distorted the view, there was certainly no doubt as to what was going on inside.

The couple were standing face to face. The woman was already stark naked and was tearing at Karl's clothes—Claire still couldn't reconcile the recipient of the other woman's lust as being *her* Karl—going at him like a death row inmate devouring a final meal. She kissed Karl with an all-consuming, hungry passion, and Claire could see her tongue slip in and out of his eager mouth, as if it were some living thing they were passing between them.

The woman—Karl's *mistress*—was petite and boyish with close cut hair, wide, brown doe-eyes and the smallest, perkiest breasts that Claire had ever seen on a grown woman. She had an unkempt, unruly bush, from which peeped delicate, pink lips that glistened wet in the rays of sunlight struggling through the motel room window.

Karl was naked now, save for his immaculately laundered, white toweling socks—always self-conscious about his feet, was Karl—his dick up and bobbing to attention. He guided the woman on to the bed, and as she spread her legs almost impossibly wide to receive his cock, she looked to Claire like some porn star, Audrey-fucking-Hepburn.

And when Karl (of *Claire'n'Karl* fame) buried his face between the woman's thighs and told her just how much he was looking forward to screwing the fuck out of her sweet asshole *again*, Claire ran away.

Claire sat in her two-hundred-thousand-dollar car in the motel parking lot and cried. Profuse tears blurred her vision, and she hawked back thick, cloying snot that clogged the back of her throat and threatened to choke her. Her mind raced this way and that; what was Karl doing in this God-awful place with some boyish-looking woman? Who *was* said boyish-looking woman? Why was Karl fucking her when he was betrothed to Claire? Such a romantic, twee word was *betrothed;* did anyone actually use it nowadays? If not, then they ought to, it's a wonderful word that promised lifetimes together, love and bliss and unerring faithfulness.

Of course, that particular irony was not lost on Claire. Nor was the fact that perhaps her own actions last night should really cancel out Karl's adultery, but somehow Karl's indiscretion seemed to be far worse to Claire than her own because his seemed all very *planned*.

Again.

She'd most definitely heard him say that he looked forward to screwing porn-Audrey Hepburn's ass *again*. Not only was this sordid fuck-fest planned, but it also wasn't the first.

How could he?

Claire wiped her eyes clear with the back of a hand. She sniffled salty, runny snot to the back of her throat and gulped it down; it felt unpleasant in her empty stomach. Perhaps she should just go home and wait for Karl there? Or could she possibly pretend that this didn't just happen and carry on as usual?

"My mother was right," she said to herself in despair. "All men *are* fucking shit."

She ignored the fresh welling of tears that threatened and gunned the engine. The Aston Martin burst into life with a deep, throaty growl.

"So, you're going to run home and cry your pussy little eyes out?" A voice chastised.

Claire turned her head and fully expected to see Randy staring back at her through the car window with that shit-eating grin on his dumb face.

No one there.

Claire wiped her eyes a second time. She returned her gaze to the door behind which Karl was going to ass-fuck some woman 'till she screamed blue murder. Apparently.

"If I were you, I'd take that gun from the glove compartment, kick that bloody door in and shoot the place up," the voice said.

"What the hell?" Claire peered frantically through the car's windows, twisted around to get a look through the rear window. Her spine crackled audibly at the effort and made her jump.

Still nothing.

Claire switched off the engine and rubbed her temples. She was clearly in no fit state to drive just now, not now that she was hearing things. She clicked open the glove compartment and eyed the small revolver that dwelled within; she'd bought it last year after an attempted carjack in Miami. It only held six bullets, but it was compact, easy to handle and fit just perfect in her purse. And besides, just how many bullets do you actually *need* to stop a carjacker?

"Then again, I'm not you," the voice said. "Obviously."

"For Christ's' sakes!" Claire shouted out loud. She clutched either side of her head and felt like she was on the brink of insanity and desperately needed all of this to just go away.

"You really do need to grow a pair and face this, you know," the voice told her. "Karl is making quite the fool out of you, my dear." This time the voice sounded as clear to Claire as if its owner were perched on her shoulder.

"What the fuck is this?" Claire's voice trembled. "Get out of my fucking head!"

"I would if I could, my dear—but I'm not in your head."

The voice spoke with a whiny British accent that reminded Claire of *someone*. Michael Caine? Austin Powers? No, it was more like Dick Van Dyke's unconvincing chimney sweep turn in that Disney movie. So, who?

Then it came to her, dredged from the dark recesses of her memory, and Claire got the mental image of the tousle-haired, English comedian with his (she was convinced) fake cockney—*mockney*—London accent. Russell Brand, that was the guy.

Claire was pleased that she'd regained enough sanity to place her hallucination's voice, although she had never found Brand particularly amusing and couldn't look at him without thinking *he's had a go on Katy Perry*.

"Couldn't be much farther from the truth, actually," the voice broke her reverie, and Claire was sure that a laugh lurked amongst the words.

It was then that Claire realized the voice appeared to be coming from the crumpled, stained sanitary bag she'd tossed into the passenger foot well.

"Holy shit." Claire stared at the bag, at the scrunched-up features of the Victorian lady.

"Not quite," the voice said with a light laugh to its timbre, "but perhaps close enough."

Gingerly, Claire picked up the bag, opened it and peered inside, convinced that she had finally stepped over the precipice to insanity. The unmistakable waft of Indian spices and stale come greeted her, and she pulled her face away with a look of disgust.

The oddest thing was that Claire could have sworn that the bag felt heavier than when she'd left the restroom, as if there was physically more crap in the bag along with her ruined panties.

"*What* the fuck are you?" Claire felt somewhat ridiculous addressing a paper bag containing her soiled underwear. But hey, when in Madtown, make like a lunatic!

"I'm the only part of you that's ever had any balls when it comes to your personal life," the voice inside the bag snarled. "Metaphorically speaking, of course."

Claire shook her head, feeling that her grip on sanity

was slipping. "I don't believe this," she said. "This really is some weird shit."

"Weird? *Really?*" The voice sounded quite put out. "Look, I'm going to let that one—and only that one—go, Claire. I'll chalk it up to your being upset right now. But please don't say it again; it really is most offensive."

"I—I'm sorry," Claire stammered, not really sure what she'd done wrong.

"Now, are we going to go and confront that cheating little shit fiancé of yours, or not?" the voice demanded. "See, now you've got me at it." It attempted at a laugh that just sounded forced. The voice didn't appear to be well versed in the art of humor. "You owe it to *Claire fucking Jepson* to at least stand up for yourself."

***

And so it was that Claire found herself back outside room 26, wearing her Chanel suit, two-thousand-dollar shoes and clutching the feminine hygiene bag. She could hear clearly the sounds of rampant, energetic sex from within the room, and it made Claire wonder when was the last time Karl had fucked *her* so damn thoroughly. Claire thrust her free hand into a jacket pocket and caressed the cool metal of the gun with trembling fingers.

"Listen to them in there. It's disgusting," the voice said.

Claire pressed her ear to the door. "Do you think of me when you're fucking her?" the woman moaned.

"Every fucking time," Karl replied, his breath labored. "It's the only way I can keep up the pretense. Shit, it's the only way I can keep *anything* up."

They laughed together.

"I thought you'd just think of the money," the woman gasped. "I'm flattered."

"There is that," Karl grunted. "And once the dumb bitch marries me, half of it's ours." He stabbed his penis into his muse a couple more times.

"Tell me what it's like when you shoot it in her mouth, Karl. Do you think about how it feels for me when I swallow you?"

"I try not to think of you when she's sucking my cock, Danielle; that would just gross me out," Karl panted. He let out a loud *ahhhhh* that drilled through Claire's brain like—well, like a fucking drill.

"Sinking into your pussy is just the most exquisite thing, like, ever, my love," Karl purred.

"And so is having your cock inside me, Karl. It's why I married you."

This revelation proved to be the last straw for Claire, the final insult to everything she held dear, Karl, love, sex, their life together. She plucked the gun from her pocket, clutched tight onto the paper bag, and shouldered the flimsy door.

"What the f—!" Karl cried out, face flushed pink from his exertions.

The woman beneath Karl squealed and attempted to wriggle free, but Karl lay frozen on top of her, and his weight pinned her down whilst his dick firmly skewered her to the lumpy mattress.

"It's not what it looks like, Claire," the cliché spilled from Karl's mouth, as he stared wide-eyed at the gun in his fiancée's shaking hand.

"It's exactly what it looks like," the British voice piped up. "You're fucking your wife. There, I explained it for you."

"E-E-Ex-wife," the woman ventured, as if that would

magically make everything okay.

"Fucking pedant," the voice replied. "And please, don't stop your buggery on my account."

Claire wiggled the gun and walked towards her lover and her lover's wife—*ex-wife*—whatever the fuck she was. She pulled the door closed behind her, easing it shut the best she could on the broken catch.

Eyes never once leaving the gun, Karl thrust into the woman as they were forced to finish their congress at gunpoint.

Claire watched the love of her life fuck the other woman with a peculiar, detached feel. She'd heard it a thousand times, but it really did feel like she was watching a movie, albeit an especially sad, cheap porn movie. She kept her eyes fixed on Karl as he ground away at his Audrey Hepburn look-a-like, and she felt neither angry nor aroused at the depressing display. *There's nothing in life much worse than sex with all of the emotions taken out of it*, she thought.

Karl finally grunted to a reluctant climax, and Claire was sure that the woman—Danielle, wasn't it?—had faked her orgasm to get the whole sorry thing over and done with as quickly and efficiently as possible. It had been the least convincing orgasm Claire thought she'd seen in a long while.

Karl rolled off of Danielle, and Claire could see that he had indeed been buried deep inside the woman's ass. There were fat, brown streaks along the sides of his cock, and she could see the vivid scarlet of prolapsed rectum between Danielle's legs. Claire watched, fascinated, as Danielle clenched the bulging organ back through her anus until it disappeared inside her like a rare, timid creature.

Karl and his ex-wife scrabbled to cover their nudity with the threadbare sheets, an action that Claire found quaint. As if that really mattered right now.

"You *decevious* little shit, Karl." Claire fought to keep her voice firm.

She watched as Karl rolled his eyes at her. She knew how much he hated it when she blended words together to make her own, which was precisely why she'd said it. It was one of his pet peeves with the woman he was supposed to love; he said she came across as thinking she was too fucking smart to use the regular words that were good enough for everyone else.

"What did I tell you?" the voice retorted

"That's offensive!"

"Who the fuck is that?" Danielle asked

"Are you some kind of freakin' ventriloquist?"

"You can hear it, too?" Claire said.

Danielle and Karl nodded in unison.

"Thank Christ for that." Claire exhaled deeply. "I thought I was going insane." She let out a wry laugh that was swiftly sucked dry in the strained atmosphere of the motel room.

Claire threw the paper bag onto the floor, positive that there was even more in the bag now than before she'd interrupted Karl's clandestine fucktime. The bag landed with a soggy plop on the faded linoleum, and they all stared down at it. There could be no mistaking its contents, as the stink from the gaily decorated bag was a dead giveaway.

"Would you mind not tossing me around, please?" The voice was painfully polite.

"What's in the bag, Claire?" Karl asked as he edged backwards on the bed. He eyed the offending article as if maybe his scorned fiancée had brought a bomb along to the party.

"It's a bag of shit," Claire told him.

"Pardon me?" Danielle said.

"I said," Claire spoke with slow deliberation, keeping

the gun trained on Danielle and Karl, "it is a bag of shit. I crapped myself on the freeway, and those are my soiled panties." She surprised herself, feeling not one twinge of embarrassment at sharing the revelation. "And now it's talking."

"Claire," Karl held out his arms, palms up, "this is a stressful situation, and it's making you a little crazy. If you would just please put the gun down, we can talk about this."

"Stressful?" Claire exploded. "I catch the man I'm about to marry in some fuck-awful shithole motel, balls-deep in his wife's butt—"

"Ex-wife." Danielle interrupted.

"Will you just shut the fuck up, bitch!" Claire cocked the gun at Danielle, and the woman cowered behind her bed sheet and shut the fuck up. "Of course, I'm going crazy, Karl, what do you expect?" Claire's voice lowered. "I heard you talking," she said. "You've been lying to me all along." She took a long, deep breath. "Have you ever loved me?"

"In my own way, I guess," Karl offered, as if that somehow justified his deceit and made everything right, like a little boy being forced to say sorry to the fat kid he'd just beaten up. Karl grinned that sexy half-grin of his that on any other occasion would have had Claire's cunt dripping like a broken fridge.

As it was, it was all Claire could do not to shoot the deceitful fuck in the face and be done with this whole unpleasant business. She did consider throwing her previous night's infidelity in Karl's face, but guessed that wouldn't have much impact on the cheating bastard and would only serve to muddy the water, so to speak. So, Claire decided to keep the moral high ground and take neither course of action.

For now.

"I can assume that everything you've said to me in the past two years has been complete crap?" Claire fought back the tears by maintaining her mental focus on the revolver. Part of her wondered whether or not she actually had the intestinal fortitude to fire the damned thing.

"Really, Claire?" The voice sounded really quite annoyed with her.

All eyes darted to the feminine hygiene bag in the middle of the room. Claire was positive now that it looked fuller than it had a few minutes ago; the Victorian lady appeared quite plump

"Claire?" Karl questioned. "Are you doing..?"

"Of course, she's not doing this," the voice chastised. "You're engaged to a software entrepreneur, not Jeff fucking Dunham!"

Claire stared forlornly at the bag and saw that it made a weird, pulsating motion as the posh British voice spoke.

"You gotta be shitting me?" Karl stared with utter disbelief.

"Will you two just quit with the references already?" The voice yelled, and its raised voice stunned Claire and Karl into slack-jawed silence. "I am *so* sick and tired of *shit-this*, *crap-that*; it's just downright offensive! And most likely racist, too! Or should that be *crappist*?"

Claire cracked a weak smile that made her look even more like a crazy person. She could see that the bag was getting bigger by the second, its paper seams straining, and the Victorian lady now appeared morbidly obese, bringing to Claire's mind the sweat-suited lard asses who hog the Wal-Mart disabled scooters – as if being a greedy bastard was ever a disability.

"Jesus H," Karl said, "this really is some fucked up shit."

"You'd better believe it, baby," the voice said with a chuckle, in what was a passable Frank-N-Furter impersonation.

"Tell me, people," the voice adopted a serious tone, "why is it that excrement always gets the bad press and derisory comments?" the voice cracked a little with emotion. "When we are a by-product of one of the human animal's greatest pleasures?"

Claire couldn't help but look at Karl, perplexed.

"People eat for sustenance, for comfort, for pleasure; hell, you even eat for fucking sport!" the voice ranted. "And in order to eat, one has to defecate, a perfectly natural bodily function. I'm sure you will agree."

Claire, Karl and Danielle nodded.

"A natural life function, which is constantly derided as filthy and disgusting." the voice continued. "And just how do you think that makes *me* feel?" The voice was raised now to deafeningly loud, and the bag pulsed like an exposed heart.

And expanded a little.

"I'll tell you how it makes me feel! It makes me feel like some dirty, revolting secret that is to be ashamed of, ignored, and hidden away like some retard relative one keeps in the basement. Every time I hear one of your fecal-related expletives, it cuts me to the quick, I can tell you!" The emotion in the voice bounced around the grimy walls like a child's screech. "You really have no fucking idea!" it stropped. "It is absolutely astounding, especially when you consider that Mother Nature made passing a stool *actually* pleasurable! Did you know that there are more nerve endings in the human anus than there are in the penis?"

Stupidly, both Claire and Karl shook their heads; no, they did not know that. Danielle just gawked in disbelief at the pair of them.

"Of course, you don't. Nobody does. And what's

more, nobody gives a shit!" the voice whined. "See, there I go again. Your contempt is infectious."

"I am so sorry," Claire said and glanced down at the bag, which was now beginning to split at the seams. She got the impression that this whole scenario had become more about the racist/crappist agenda of her—the—whatever the fuck the thing was in the rapidly expanding bag.

"You're actually apologizing to it?" Karl was incredulous. "You're talking to shit, Claire! You're fucking crazy!"

"But you hear it, too, Karl." Claire aimed the gun at his head; one squeeze of the trigger and the boyish Danielle and her perky little tits would be wearing her ex-husband's brains.

"It could be mass hysteria." Karl sounded desperate.

"There are only three of us in here, Karl." Claire's voice was calm. "How can it be *mass* anything?"

"So, are you going to do the right thing or not?" The voice, directed at Claire, sounded caustic.

"The right thing?" Claire enquired and squinted at the revolver. "Yeah, sure." She fixed her eyes squarely on Karl's down the gun barrel. "Karl," She said as calmly as she could manage, "I think it's safe to assume that we're through."

"That's it?" the voice exploded. "That's fucking it? He conspires with his ex-wife to string you along for two years, gets you to fall head over heels and make plans to marry so he can get his greedy hands on your money - and it's *we're through*!" The voice cracked into a shrill, mocking laugh. "I'm beginning to think that you deserve all of this, Claire!"

"I do *not* deserve any of this," Claire growled.

"They targeted you, Claire. They picked you out—of the business pages for all you know—as prey," the voice spewed its venom. "And let's face it; with your lack of social skills, repressed memories of the bullying you experienced at school, *and* inherent guilt about your supposedly secret bisexuality, you were an easy target."

"It wasn't like that!" Karl butted in, he sounded increasingly desperate. "I liked you from the get-go, Claire. It was her who planned the scam." He nodded his head towards a shocked Danielle.

"Why don't you just shut the whiny little fucker up, Claire?" the voice demanded. "What kind of turd throws his own under the bus the second there's a gun in his face?" The bag appeared dangerously full now, and with each pulse, it threatened to tear wide open.

"I loved you, Karl," Claire sniffled. "I really did."

"Stop being so damned pathetic," the voice admonished. "Your entire relationship has been a complete fabrication. All the times you made love, he was gritting his teeth and thinking about his small-titted wifey and your hard-earned cash. If that happened to me, I'd *want* to kill someone!"

"Yeah, you're right," Claire snarled.

"So, pull the fucking trigger!"

Claire took a step forward.

"No!" Karl shuffled back farther on the bed and instinctively pulled the grubby sheet tight around his body, as if the appallingly low thread count could stop a bullet. "I'm sorry, Claire."

"Sorry?" The voice mocked. "You can't let him get away with *sorry*!"

"You fucking hurt me, Karl." Claire felt the first of her fresh tears drip down her cheek. "This—us—the whole thing. How could you?"

"Never mind that, finish him—now!" the voice shouted.

"I should..." Claire replied.

"Look at your unfaithful fiancé, naked in bed with the conspiratorial wife he never told you he had!" The voice dug at the truth. "For Christ's sakes, he's still got her shit on his prick!"

"You're a bastard, Karl." Claire's finger caressed the cold steel of the trigger.

"That's it, Claire!" the voice encouraged. "Shoot the asshole right between his lying eyes!"

"Yeah!" Claire's voice boomed. "You *decevious* piece of shit, Karl!" Another step forward, a little more pressure on the trigger.

"That's it Claire..," the absolute glee in the voice's tone was undisguised.

Claire closed her eyes, braced herself for the sharp report and the recoil that she knew from her gun training to expect.

Lowered the gun.

"I can't," Claire cried.

The feminine hygiene bag ripped itself apart; a ragged tear in the flimsy paper spliced the poor Victorian lady in two. A brown, bubbling mass leapt out from the bag and rapidly expanded in volume, as it hurtled towards the bed and its horrified occupants. As the disgusting mess shot by Claire, it filled the dank air in the motel room with an all-too familiar stench.

Claire stepped back, struggling to believe what she was witnessing. The voluminous mess from the bag had formed into a huge, amorphous blob of oozing, brown shit that was, in an instant, as big as—no, half as big again as—a grown man. And Claire could swear that somewhere within its shifting configuration she could make out the vague yet discernible shape of something unnatural and otherworldly.

The sickening brown mass fell upon Karl in what must have been the ultimate brown shower. It smothered Karl as he writhed and bucked on the bed, the thick chocolate-colored slime crawled up into his mouth and nose. Karl clawed at the suffocating excrement to no avail, unable to tear it away as its substance was too mercurial, too insubstantial for his fingers to gain purchase.

Claire stood as transfixed as she was horrified; the dull stench of putrefaction clung to her like a terrible coat, and she could see that everywhere the stuff touched Karl's naked flesh it bubbled and fizzed and disintegrated.

And out of it slithered fat, oozing tendrils that looked like hellish, blind snakes. They writhed and slid over and around Karl whilst some fashioned wicked, keen claws at their tips, which they then used to slice and stab at his exposed flesh. Others carved their way up into his ass, and viscous, dark blood poured out behind them.

Covered head to toe with the oozing, morphing mess, Karl screamed his stifled screams through the feces that clogged up his windpipe and sputtered back up through his lipless mouth. He continued to claw and scrape, even though his fingers were digested down to their bones.

Soon, Karl's agonized thrashing grew weak. The shit-blob shot out a slender tendril and curled it around Karl's cheating dick, which it quickly dissolved into a pinkish-gray slime. Karl gave out one final, ululating yowl and kicked out his feet in a hanging-man's spasm.

One of Karl's flailing feet kicked Danielle hard in the ribs, and this seemed to spur her into action. Bare-assed naked, the panicking girl scrambled from the bed and made a break for the door.

A glob of shit broke away from Karl and slid after Danielle, like some obscene, brown amoeba. From it, there erupted a pair of thick excrement ropes, which wrapped themselves around Danielle's legs and brought her down like a snared rabbit. She screamed as the shit crawled over her and forced itself down her throat and sent a triumvirate of tendrils up along her thigh to explore and probe at her vagina, pee hole, and anus.

As the brown entity went to work on Danielle with busy, digestive tendrils and sharp, vicious claws, Claire couldn't help but notice that as Danielle's body was broken down, her assailant became increasingly more solid and was beginning to take on the approximation of a recognizable shape.

It was becoming more *human*.

Claire watched Danielle's mute protests with more than a twinge or two of pleasure, as the woman ripped out her own throat in her vain fight for breath. An arc of bright, arterial blood reached to the ceiling and sprayed it red. Together with the spattered feces, it looked like a Jackson Pollock masterpiece.

Danielle's twisted, dissolving face – almost already down to the glinting white of skull bone—was largely largely concealed by a mask of pulsing, congealing shit, and her one remaining eye stared out at Claire, as if begging her to please make this all stop.

As if Claire would if she could.

As Danielle died, choking on Claire's shit, Karl flopped from the bed with a final burst of life. His body was wasted, his bones and organs protruded through the shifting, seeping brown slime, and Claire could make out a peculiar gurgling sound that seemed to be coming from deep in his chest. It sounded to Claire like he was saying her name. He crawled towards his fiancée, frantic fingers scrabbling on the slick floor, his eyes wide and imploring.

Karl died at Claire's feet.

All fell silent. The stuff from the bag—Claire still struggled to concede as to what it actually was—lay spattered and pulsing next to Danielle's ravaged corpse. Its spatters and smears were on every conceivable surface of the motel room, painting a grim testimony to the unspeakable demise of the deceitful, devious Karl and his ex-wife. The mess moved with slow deliberate actions and seemed to be pulling the scattered parts of itself back together on the naked corpses of Karl and his porn-Audrey Hepburn, as it slithered across the floor to feast some more on the death it had created.

A corpulent shit-rope snaked out from the seething mess and made its way purposefully towards Claire. It flattened itself out and rose up to head height, an arm's length away. And as the shifting, semi-liquid stuff swirled and formed and unformed again, Claire thought that she could see a face.

"Holy fucking shit," Claire muttered to herself and leveled her gun at the abomination before her.

***

The cop held a booger-encrusted handkerchief to his nose and made a mental note to retire the monogrammed cotton germ-factory to the laundry at the end of his shift. It was a necessary precaution against the stink that emanated from the motel room behind him, which was execrable, even though he was standing outside and had the relief of the relatively fresh outdoor air. Just his fucking luck to be First on Scene, he grumbled to himself; now he had to stick around until the M.E. had finished poking around.

The cop stared down at his shoes in disgust. They were smeared and splashed with caking globs of runny shit, right up to the goddamn lace holes. He'd stepped on a sodden paper bag when he'd first arrived at the motel room and was trying to check the victims for signs of life. This was before it became patently obvious that they were both beyond help in this world. The bag had contained a pair of lace panties and an ungodly amount of shit, the latter of which had squished up his shoes as he trod on it. *Perhaps*, the cop thought to himself, *I should throw the shoes away and put in an expense claim for a new pair.*

The motel manager, a fat, greasy character by the name of Randy, had called it in after he'd heard shots. Sadly, by the time the cop had arrived, the excitement was all over and done with.

The cop figured that it would be a long time—if ever—before he would be able to erase the memories of what he'd seen in room 26; there were some things that you simply couldn't un-see. A pair of naked bodies that looked like they'd been pulled out of a shallow grave after three months of rotting, and a blood and shit smeared motel room were most definitely in that category.

Most likely some kind of sick sex game gone terribly wrong, the cop reckoned. He'd seen some German scat porn on the Internet, and he guessed that the two stiffs in the room had met up for a little shit-play here. Although, it was beyond him as to what could possibly have gone so spectacularly wrong, and to just how long the corpses had lain there with nobody bothering to report the stink.

"Hey, Andy." The Medical Examiner strode across the parking lot and broke the cop's reverie. He wrinkled his nose at the stench that wafted from the room.

"Hi," the cop replied, his mind still elsewhere.

"This the one?"

The cop nodded. "Prepare yourself, Doc, there's some real weird shit gone down in there."

"*Weird shit?* Really?" An indignant voice came from inside the motel room, and the cop thought it sounded British.

TWO

At around the same time as Claire Jepson was racing home from Randy's Motel—*sans* underwear and mind fit to burst—to clean herself up, relieve her aching bowels once more, and get back to her office for the monthly board meeting, Tony and Krystal Wyatt along with their fuckbuddy, Samuel Nester were eying up the prospective 'talent' at the *Exclusive Triple-X Adult Theater* (open 24/7).

Had anyone there cared enough to take note, the trio stood out from the regular clientele like the proverbial sore thumbs. Samuel wore expensive, fashionably distressed 501's and a black T-shirt that showed off his bulging muscles, and Tony wore crisp Chinos and a designer polo shirt worth more than the theater made in a month. Krystal was closest to adult theater attire with her butt-skimming denim skirt and scarlet halter top that showed off her huge, bra-less tits to perfection, although her outfit did say *new,* and her Manolo Blahnik heels screamed money.

Far from being exclusive, the *Triple-X* was a grubby fleapit porn theater secreted at the rear of a questionable sex shop on the rougher edge of town. It was a favorite hangout for those less discerning amongst the town's swinging community, along with pretty much anyone else who liked their sexual thrills cheap and nasty.

Tony, Krystal and Samuel knew through experience that pickings were generally slim this early in the day, but today there was an unusually good mix of lowlifes on offer. There were the halfway house, unemployable types—three today—who came in to get low-cost thrills and to escape the oppressive Texas heat outside. Whilst the theater was air conditioned, the management tended to keep the inside temperature in the high seventies to encourage spontaneous nudity amongst its pleasure-seeking patrons in the forty-seat cinema, but it was still a welcome comfort from the ninety degrees plus outside. For just five bucks (ladies free, of course) the ex-crackheads got to stay cool all day, watch some cheesy, nineteen-eighties pornography, and entertain at least the hope of getting a little action. Having said that, for the majority of the haggard-faced men who frequented the joint, *action* was pretty much a masturbatory affair.

Sitting in the back row of the movies—*hey, wasn't that a Drifters' song?* Samuel had asked Tony—were a couple of middle-aged, plumpish guys who looked disturbingly like they could be brothers. They watched, stone-faced and wide-eyed, the lackluster action up on the screen as they gingerly jerked each other off under a grubby, plaid blanket, which looked for all the world like someone's Meemaw had knitted it. Tony had found it incredible to think that one (or both?) of the men had purposefully brought said *blankie* along to a sex cinema.

And that made the chubby brothers' dirty tryst all the more sordid.

On the front row of the theater a nude, meth-head

skank with dirty blonde hair and rotted features was dishing out blowjobs for ten bucks a go. And business was brisk. Currently, she was busy bringing a skinny guy in a U-of-H T-shirt and cut off jeans shorts to completion.

From where he stood, Tony could see her gulping the guy's come down her scrawny throat and figured that it was probably the first decent meal she'd had in days. Behind that client stood another two—older guys whose heads blocked off part of the bottom of the screen. They had small wads of money clutched in their sweaty hands and eager smiles on their faces; they'd look just like kids lining up at an ice cream truck, were it not for the hirsute vaginas that were being projected onto their thinning scalps.

The trio watched Meth-Whore going about her business with more interest than they afforded the badly dubbed action on screen. There, a thirty-something Asian lady with a sad face and National Geographic breasts was taking double anal from a couple of averagely hung white guys. They'd over-dubbed Asian Woman's pained cries for moans of ecstasy; one look at the poor woman's contorted face was enough to see that she was, in fact, in a considerable amount of discomfort.

Meth-Whore was as skinny as one would have expected for a seasoned addict. Her shoulder blades and angular hip bones stuck out beneath taut, pallid skin, her knees and elbows looked like thick, bony knots and the knobbles of her spine were sharp and prominent. Tony thought she looked like some kind of exotic lizard. Her wasted frame—complete with the deflated breasts that clung to the protruding rack of her rib cage—reeked to high heaven of her poison of choice, and the stink clung to her like cloying L.A.

smog, her lank hair thick with it. When she broke off from her client and ushered him away, Tony and the others could see that most of the woman's teeth were missing, and those that remained - clinging like limpets to an oil-ruined shore—were broken and jagged and an unnaturally dark gray. Her youngish face—they guessed her at no more than early thirties—had a sickly, waxy sheen and was ravaged with deep, dirty lines and dotted with weeping sores that only a decade or so of methamphetamine abuse can provide.

Tony, Krystal and Samuel knew—also from experience—that Meth-Whore was actually named Susan (*never* Sue) and that she also offered a full-on fuck for twenty-five bucks. But, sweet Jesus, who would want to go *there*?

Well, they would, for starters. Such was their bizarre life.

The Wyatts had been married for six years and change when Krystal had introduced Samuel to the marital bed. At first, she had forced Tony to sit and watch as she rode Samuel's magnificent cock, and she had taken great delight in her cuckold husband's discomfort. She would screw Samuel hard and fast, sitting astride the thick meat of his thighs, bouncing her fat, pendulous breasts and pulling on the dark pink of her cookie-sized nipples that covered the entire end of each tit.

Sure, it was almost too clichéd to be a cliché, but Krystal had always fantasized about having an affair with a black guy, and from the first time Samuel squeezed—no, *forced*—the fat, pink tip of his monster penis into her tight pussy, she knew she would never be able to give him up. But she was still madly in love with Tony—*her* Tony with his pale, skinny body and slicked down cap of ginger hair, and she was too damned selfish to give *him* up either.

So, Krystal had brought Samuel into her marriage as nothing more than a sex toy. Then, she had gradually insinuated him more and more into her and Tony's life until he was pretty much a permanent fixture both in bed and out of it.

For his part, Tony had understood from the off that he had two choices with his wife's arrangement, and one of those choices was to walk. Since he had no desire to be without the love of his life and her beautiful, curvaceous body and insatiable appetite of all things perverted, Tony had made the decision to accept the arrangement as his lot and had learned to appreciate the exciting new addition to his sex life.

He and Samuel had eased into their expected roles with some light sword fencing, which had quickly extended to double-teaming Krystal on a regular basis—one in the cunt, one in the ass. Tony's preference was always Krystal's ass, and he'd grown fond of the sensation of Samuel's thick dick rubbing against his own through the thin membranes that separated his wife's pussy from her deliciously tight corn-hole.

On Krystal's designated bi-nights, Tony and Samuel would suck and fuck, naked and sweating on the bed while Krystal rubbed furiously at her clit like she was trying to erase it. Reluctant at first, it was now something that Tony rather looked forward to.

If someone had told Tony Wyatt three years ago that he would be in a three-way marriage and that he would love the feel of another man's cock stretching both his lips and his ass wide open, he'd have called them crazy to their crazy-ass faces.

Tony chose to view it as having the best of both worlds, of three worlds if he *really* thought about it. He was married to the most vibrant and sexually uninhibited woman on the planet. He had an enviably varied sex life in which he could entertain his erstwhile latent bisexual tendencies, and he had free reign to explore every sexual deviation he cared to have a go at. It was like living life in a top-quality porn film, and it was a most pleasant and welcome distraction from the hectic hubbub of their everyday lives.

Krystal was a pediatric doctor in a bustling city hospital, which is where she'd met Tony. He'd been transferred in from New York to head the cardio-thoracic team and had enjoyed a meteoric rise to become one of the country's best heart surgeons—and in record time, too.

Samuel—the odd one out of the trio, professionally speaking—was a wealth management specialist who Krystal had bumped into at a rich swingers' party in a downtown loft apartment. She'd been on her way to the restroom with an eye full of stinging come—an occupational hazard for the bukkake slut she'd been at the time—and he'd kindly helped her rinse it out. Once her vision had returned, she'd introduced Samuel to Tony, and they'd all taken turns fucking each other in the love-swing.

Of course, slumming it together in seedy sex cinemas was not their only vice, it was just one in a growing catalog of low down, dirty activities that they got themselves involved in, specifically to court distraction and garner cheap thrills.

In recent years, Krystal, Tony and Samuel had beaten people up for gang money (they knew the kind of people who paid people like them to do their dirty work, and they had been more than happy to oblige), kidnapped people, stolen high-end motor vehicles to order (again, they knew the people...), and had stuffed their orifices full of Category A substances and taken international flights as hired drug mules.

There'd been the scare nine months ago when a condom—ribbed for her pleasure—filled with five ounces of the purest Columbian had sprung a leak in Krystal's vagina at thirty-thousand feet. The near disaster had been Krystal's own fault as she had been locked in the cramped 737 rest room with the co-pilot at the time. She'd been jerking him off between her pussy lips, and he'd gotten a little too enthusiastic and despite her warnings, had slipped his dick into her hole with an almighty thrust.

It was lucky that Krystal had recognized the early symptoms of OD and fished the drugs out before any permanent damage was done to her system. She'd thrown the co-pilot out beforehand, of course, and then simply wrapped the drugs inside the spare rubber she kept in her purse and pushed it right back up inside her cunt to rejoin with its compadres.

All in all, it was a full and varied life that the three enjoyed together; pretty much the only thing they hadn't done to date was to kill someone. That was not because of the Hippocratic Oath that two of the unholy trio had signed back in med' school, but simply because that particular opportunity had not presented itself.

Yet.

Which brings Krystal, Tony and Samuel back to the Triple-X Theater (*open 24/7*), where they were awaiting a phone call to green-light their next assignment and killing time the best way they knew how.

"I double-dog dare you." Krystal whispered to Tony and nodded towards Meth-Whore.

The disgusting wreck of womanhood was just finishing off the final client in her sad line-up, and the final spurt of his cock-juice dribbled from her ruined mouth. She looked over at the trio and smiled her snaggle-toothed smile as if she knew full well that she was the subject of their next dare.

"Well, if it's a double-dog dare." Tony smiled at her. As if he would even consider refusing the challenge. He made his way in the semi-dark down the aisle to the woman, his shoes sticking to the tacky carpet as he walked with Krystal and Samuel following close behind; Krystal had removed her vertiginous shoes and was now regretting it as some of the patches on the burgundy patterned carpet were still wet and something nasty squidged up between her toes.

"You sure?" Samuel, as ever the more cautious of the three. He peered through the gloom at the unfortunate woman who now knelt alone in front of the flickering screen. "She looks pretty rank to me."

They approached Meth-Whore. She smiled up at them, and they caught sight of her raw, chemical-burned gums and charred stubs of broken teeth. She pulled on her nipples and stretched out her flat, flaccid tits towards Tony, as if trying to bring them back to some semblance of life.

"Twenty-five?" Krystal broke the silence.

"Yep," Meth-Whore replied and the waft of her breath—meth, cheap cigarettes, ejaculate—nearly felled all three of them.

"For my husband." Krystal handed over five notes.

Meth-Whore snatched the cash from Krystal's hand as if her life, and not just her next fix, depended upon it. She scrunched the notes into a filthy tennis shoe she kept by her side, where it nestled with the rest of her day's takings. Her money shoe appeared as battered and worn out as its owner and sported a gaping hole in the toe that seemed to grin up at Krystal and her concubines with malevolence.

Meth-Whore then lay down on the sticky carpet and parted her legs, and she was illuminated in all her glory by the shining skin tones of the frantically copulating people up on the screen.

"Sweet mother of God," Samuel gasped.

"I'm saying." Tony licked his lips as he peered down

at the mess between the woman's thighs. Scabs and open sores covered almost every inch of her syphilitic cunt; some were old and crusted over while others were fresher and seeped a thin, watery liquid that was streaked with blood and a yellow-green pus. Tony felt a stirring in his loins as his body pumped its blood there, and his dick stiffened.

Krystal unbuckled Tony's pants and slid them down his skinny legs along with his underwear. His formidable cock sprung out and to attention as if Meth-Whore was quite simply the most delectable creature he'd ever had the privilege to lay his eyes upon.

Krystal's hand was damp with sweat as she wrapped it around her husband's dick to give it a gentle tug in the direction of the reclining woman, as if giving her permission for him to venture forth.

For Tony, the sight of the addict's suppurating vagina churned his stomach, which threatened to regurgitate the Denny's breakfast he'd enjoyed not two hours before. Yet somehow, that same nausea added to the frisson of the anticipated coupling. Tony swallowed hard and sank to his knees, his throbbing cock aimed at where he guessed Meth-Whore's hole to be. The scabs, he thought, would make for extra stimulation—for which he knew he'd be grateful once he got started—and the septic seepage much needed lubrication. He'd most certainly be prescribing himself a dose of industrial-strength *Gentamicin* the second he got into work tomorrow morning.

Spurred on by the groans of encouragement from his wife and Samuel, Tony inched his dick up into the Meth-Whore's diseased pussy. As he did so, his cock peeled the top off of a handful of ripe scabs as it disappeared inside her rotting body, and he could feel them scraping against his sensitive skin. Meth-Whore wriggled around a bit and made exaggerated groaning noises as she faked—badly—the throes of ecstasy.

Tony humped, joylessly, away at the woman's parched vagina and doubted very much if the recipient of his efforts was feeling much at all through the ravages of her disease. Still, pussy is pussy, he told himself and Krystal and Samuel seemed to be enjoying the show.

Samuel seated himself on one of the front row, drop-down seats with his pants down at his ankles. He lowered Krystal onto his erection with her back to him so that she could watch Tony in action as Samuel's girthsome dick slid deep inside her moist pussy. And so Tony could look up and watch her fucking.

Tony noticed that the blanket guys had moved three rows down towards the front of the theater in order to better see the impromptu sex show that had unfolded before them. He could also see that their hands were moving ever more frantically beneath the blanket. A couple of the bearded, bedraggled crackheads approached Krystal, as she ground her genitals on Samuel's with wet, slurping sounds; the guys had their dicks in hand and an optimistic grin on their sallow faces.

If they were lucky, Tony thought to himself, Krystal would suck them both off while Samuel pumped away at her, and she'd allow them to come on her angelic face. Then she'd most likely drive home with their come drying on her face and make an excuse to stop at the convenience store on the way.

That thought brought Tony to his orgasm's edge, in spite of Meth-Whore who had given up on any pretense of enjoying the act and just lay there staring off into the middle distance over Tony's shoulder.

A cell phone rang out; a stark, electronic emulation of those old-style phones that had a rotary dial.

Krystal answered. "Hi. Yeah. Okay," she grunted into

her iPhone as Samuel continued to thrust into her. "Consider it done," she said with a throaty growl as Samuel's cock hit the extra-sensitive part near her bladder. She was about to hang up the phone, but instead, she balanced it on the next seat along with the pinprick microphone hole pointing directly at her vagina. *Let 'em listen*, she thought.

Krystal then took her weight on her own formidable thighs and quickened her pace on Samuel's dick. She thrust one hand between her legs and had her fingers work enthusiastically at her clitoris to hurry things along. Occasionally, she'd slide a couple of the slippery digits inside her vagina to grab some juice and to tickle Samuel along.

"Okay, guys, the money's in our account," she said with a gasp. "It looks like we're on."

Samuel grunted in her ear and drove his dick roughly against the hard nub of her cervix as he began to come.

"No problem," Tony grunted, damned close to filling Meth-Whore with a fluid ounce or two of his own bodily fluids, "give me two."

THREE

Hayley Barnett stared at the black, plastic speaker that sat in the center of the mahogany table with a look of disgusted fascination on her pinched face. The sounds of Krystal Wyatt's embellished (it had to be, *right*?) orgasm echoed around the boardroom. It was accompanied by the noises of Tony and Samuel's exertions and the tinny cries of *fuck me!* and *harder!* and *oh yes, yes, yes!* from the porn movie that played in the background, which served to exacerbate the perverse enthrallment.

Edson Garcia leaned across the table and hit the *off* button to hang up the call to Krystal and her cohorts. Hayley shot him a look that was part *thank you,* part *how dare you!?* She'd been mesmerized by the sounds of unfettered sex that oozed from the speaker and fairly dripped from the walls; they were precisely the type of sounds that accompanied her fantasies on the long, lonely nights in the bed that she shared with no one. And much to her chagrin, as disgusted as she tried to be at the wet slurping sounds of Krystal's pussy getting crammed full of dick, she'd found herself getting more than a little damp between the legs.

Trust the gay guy to get all offended and spoil it, she fumed to herself. *If it had been a call from a guy in a gay sauna, there was no doubt at all that they'd all have had to listen through it to the inevitable end. What precisely did Edson have against vaginas anyways?*

Hayley glanced at the third member of the board and her fellow partner in crime for support. Farid Saemi, for his part, gave her no such thing. He was the oldest, the nerviest of the three odd bedfellows, and he kept his nose stuck firmly in the sheaf of paperwork he'd brought along to present to their CEO, if she ever turned up.

Hayley had been Chief Financial Officer of Jepson Software Solutions LLC for almost eight years. She was early forties, not unattractive, single, slightly on the plump side (not entirely unrelated to that tick in the '*single*' category) and considered herself to be a woman of simple tastes. She'd left a crappy, dead-end job as accountant for some monstrous, faceless corporation in Miami to join Claire's team and had for the most part not regretted the move; she was paid well, and the job was not overly demanding.

However, Hayley had to tolerate—with a smile and good grace—Claire Jepson and her demanding, narcissistic, bullying behavior that over the years had eaten into Hayley's self-esteem, to the point that she now second-guessed every piece of work she turned out. Still, the money was twice what she could ever have hoped to earn elsewhere, which some days was more of a curse than a blessing.

The kidnap plot had been all Hayley's idea, of which she was particularly proud. It had taken her some time—and a great deal of care—to persuade

Edson and Farid to work with her on it. Eventually, they had come around after Claire had had yet another meltdown and pissed off their second biggest client to the tune of two-hundred million dollars' worth of business. Claire Jepson may well have been the creative brain behind the products that had catapulted the company into the fiscal stratosphere, but her people skills were somewhat lacking. And that, according to Hayley, is what would inevitably implode the company and put them all out on the streets.

It would be easy; she'd explained over tacos. They'd stage Claire's fake kidnap and the board—the three of them—would sign off on the ransom demand. Using that money, they would buy up enough shares to mount a backdoor coup and take control of the business. If Ms. Jepson just happened to expire in the process, then, as the saying goes: Shit happens, and then you die.

Yes, Hayley Barnett had created a plan so simplistic as to be poetic, beautiful even. What could possibly go wrong?

"It's happening then?" Garcia broke the silence. "I'm still not entirely convinced…"

"Really, Edson?" Farid growled and his deep, brown eyes glowered at the Executive Vice President over wire-framed spectacles. "It's a bit fucking late for second thoughts now."

He pronounced the expletive *foooking*, which Hayley had always found cute. "Farid's right," she threw in, "it's all systems go. From this point on, we all have to make sure we stick together."

Garcia flushed a pale puce and mumbled something about being bullied into the whole thing. He shuffled his meager stack of papers and pretended to be busy.

The door flew open, and Claire Jepson breezed in. Her hair was still damp and plastered down on her scalp from the record-time shower she'd taken at home (under more normal circumstances, Claire liked to take her time bathing as she enjoyed playing the shower head's strong jets against her clitoris until she came good and hard). She wafted by her board members on the scent of patchouli and jasmine from her hundred-dollar a bottle body wash. It was a little sickly for her tastes, but anything had to be better than the pervading stink of her own mess that had followed her home from the motel, which still clung to the soft leather interior of the Aston. Because of the latter, she'd changed cars, as well as clothes, and driven to the office in the Range Rover, its new car smell an absolute relief.

"Sorry I'm late, guys. Something unavoidable came up that needed my attention," she said, as if keeping her board waiting for two hours was nothing. "Well, we'd better get started, *tempus fugit,* and all that." Claire plonked herself down in the black leather chair at the head of the table. The chair creaked and made farty noises that were a little too close to home for Claire's liking. She slapped her briefcase down on the table and pulled out a bundle of paperwork. "Okay," she said, "looks like you're up first, Hayley." She gave her financial whiz what was meant to be a friendly smile but came across as menacing.

As Hayley droned on about fiscal responsibilities this, year-on-year growth that, and decline in the industry the other, Claire eyed each one of her Board with suspicion. Out of the three, she'd fucked two of them. Claire had enjoyed Hayley's pale, doughy flesh and her rookie eagerness in bed but couldn't quite get past Hayley's one blue eye, one brown eye thing for a repeat performance; all she had been able to think of during their clumsy, sweaty coupling was that Hayley had somehow not quite been *completed;* as if her odd eyes were the result of some biological oversight. The odd man out was the all too-gay Garcia, (although not through lack of effort on Claire's part), whilst Farid had been a quickie in the stationary cupboard one Christmas that had been over so soon that it hardly counted at all.

Claire knew the three of them well enough to know that they were up to something, but she just couldn't fathom quite what. She'd noticed a subtle shift in their attitude of late; they seemed to her to be a little too willing to accept her erratic behavior with good grace and a disingenuous smile as opposed to their usual vehement arguments or a loud sigh and roll of the eyes. Nowadays, they wouldn't say boo to a fucking goose; not one of them. All of this was leading Claire to believe that whatever it was they were up to, they were in it as a threesome.

Claire Jepson's people skills were not quite as stunted as she led people to believe.

She also knew damn well that they wouldn't—couldn't—quit, simply because she paid them all well above industry standard and therefore owned their sorry asses. And they certainly couldn't buy her out or stage a hostile takeover because she didn't pay them *that* well. So, what was it to be, lady and gentlemen? Claire wondered.

Claire was brought back from her reverie, and into Hayley's increasingly dull *state of the company* presentation, by an all too familiar gurgling in the depths of her gut.

"Oh no," she grumbled beneath her breath.

"I'm sorry, Claire." Hayley looked worried.

"All I said was that the last fiscal quarter's net margin was down by 3.4 percent. It's not as bad as it looks if you take into account…"

"It's okay." Claire didn't hide her impatience. "Just carry on, and let's get through this." She rubbed at the sore spot just below her skirt's waistband and felt the building bubbles of gas churn away in there like busted Jacuzzi jets.

She could feel a sour sweat break out on her forehead and in her armpits, defying the fresh sheen of antiperspirant she'd applied, and her underarms felt damp and sticky. For the second time that day, Claire felt as if she really needed to *go*. But she could hardly excuse herself five minutes after she'd turned up late for the meeting, owner of the company or not. So, Claire sat still and quiet and focused her mind away from the discomfort that brewed in her gut.

Hayley continued on and Claire struggled to concentrate with the dull ache throbbing in her abdomen that served to remind her of two things; *one*, that she really, really ought to lay off the Indian cuisine; and *two*, that her colon wasn't quite finished with her just yet.

The fart that followed took Claire and her board members completely by surprise. No warning, no opportunity for the clenching of muscles to prevent escape. Just an elongated, resounding squeak that sounded like someone in the room had stepped on an oversized mouse.

Claire's face flushed bright red, and she suppressed a childish giggle. No one in the room said anything or dared laugh because Claire was the boss of this multi-multi million-dollar company, and she held their mortgages, car payments, bank loans—their whole fucking sad lives—in the palm of her self-obsessed hand.

Hayley carried on with her presentation as if nothing had happened while Farid and Edson studied her with intent and fought the urge to crack up laughing.

Claire shifted in her seat and discovered that she had not gotten rid of the entirety of her curry at Randy's Motel or at home and that, once again, there had been a certain amount of follow-through. She could feel the warm semi-liquid oozing between her butt cheeks and into her cotton panties. It squelched upwards along her vulva slit and felt surprisingly—and disturbingly—delightful. From the feel of it, the stuff was already soaking through Claire's Chanel skirt and on to her executive chair.

Not again, she groaned to herself.

"I am so sorry, guys. Claire stuttered. "I've, err, I've not been feeling so good." She stood up and tried her best not to look like a Chief Executive Officer/Company Owner who had just crapped in her panties. "Please excuse me, I'll be right back." She waddled from the boardroom looking like some lame penguin and hoped to dear God that her gusset would hold the flow until she reached the restroom.

And behind her, she heard the first howl of suppressed laughter from the Jepson Software Solution's Board.

"That was fucking hilarious!" Hayley blurted out as the boardroom door closed with a resolute thump. "The high and mighty Claire Jepson just shat herself!" Tears rolled down her chubby, white cheeks and streaked them sooty black with the conservative amount of mascara she allowed herself to wear.

"She's left us in the Godamm stink, though," Edson Garcia guffawed. "Smells like Miss Jepson's been eating Indian again. The food, I mean." He roared at his own risqué *double entendre*.

"That's racist, man," Farid joined in with faux offence. "But, yeah, it does remind me a little of home." He laughed along; surprised at himself with how quickly he'd succumbed to the juvenile lavatory humor.

"I thought she couldn't touch spicy foods, because of her IBS?" Garcia said between giggles and made air quotes around '*IBS*'.

"That's just something she tells people," Hayley

informed. "There's nothing wrong with the bitch, she just likes to play for the sympathy vote." Malice laced her words. "It's like me and jalapeños. I'm a little sensitive, but I love 'em and still eat them on occasion. It's a calculated risk, but at least I know well enough to make sure I'm never going to be in company or too far from a toilet the next day." She laughed.

"You are so nasty, girl!" Garcia play-slapped Hayley's hand across the table and then coughed at the cloying aroma that emanated from Claire's seat and clung to the back of his throat.

"With a bit of luck this means she'll go home early, and we can get *our* ball rolling." Hayley regained some composure. "Our people will be in place in a half hour."

This had the effect of quelling the mirth. Suddenly shit was getting very real and very scary.

Farid pursed his lips and made a fart sound. It was an accurate enough emulation of Claire's squeaky fart, and it got them all laughing again.

"You think it's funny, do you?" A disembodied voice silenced the laughter.

Hayley looked around, wide-eyed with fear. She caught the others' eyes and saw the fear ensconced in them.

"Did she bug the place?" Hayley whispered.

Farid and Garcia shook their heads, more as if to say *I don't know* than *no*, but too terrified to speak, just in case.

"Would you find it all so fucking funny if Ms. Jepson knew that you were planning to have her killed?" The voice seemed to be coming from everywhere and nowhere and sounded to Hayley like some of the less savory characters she enjoyed when she binge-watched *Eastenders* on BBC America.

Hayley twisted her head this way and that, desperately looking for the speaker that common sense told her *had* to be hidden somewhere in the office, although she was not sure how she'd actually see one if there was. Her mind conjured up images of Claire sitting in the security office watching her Board squirm in the knowledge that she had exposed their treachery. That and having a little fun of her own, toying with them by using the voice distortion software that they'd developed years ago.

She noted, too, that the reek of effluent in the room had become almost tangible; it hung thick and sickly in the air like the stink of death in an abattoir.

"Well, I, for one, am not laughing," the voice boomed.

Farid struggled to his feet, and his dickey hip clicked loudly as it threatened to give way and dump him on the floor.

"She's on to us. We have to get out of here," he said, somewhat unnecessarily as he made for the door. He stopped dead in his tracks when he saw the sizable brown shape that was arising from Claire Jepson's chair.

"Holy crap..." he stammered.

"Less of the holy, Mr. Farid, if you don't mind." The voice dripped from the shape that now seemed to have formed itself into a rough outline of something vaguely human.

Hayley and Garcia wheeled their chairs towards the back of the boardroom to be away from the oozing, brown mass and the stomach-churning stench that emanated from it.

Farid made another dash for the door, but the stinking thing was quicker than anticipated, and it made it to the door at the same time. Farid's instinctive, primal revulsion towards all things fecal caused him to hesitate for a fraction of a second, and that was to be his undoing.

A horde of writhing, shifting tendrils erupted from the

excrement and shot out towards Farid. He tried to scream, but a triad of thick, slimy brown ropes filled his mouth and slithered down his throat. The longest of the tendrils gripped his body like stinking, malevolent fingers and held him in a lover's embrace that drew him ever closer into the seething wall of putrescence. And everywhere the stuff touched Farid's skin, his flesh frothed and dissolved, as if by acid. Simultaneously, yet more of those terrible, slippery fingers formed razor keen claws at their tips and began tearing at him.

Farid did his very best to wriggle free, but the grasp of the shit-tendrils was one of preternatural strength and more and more of the oily snakes invaded his body through every orifice they could find; he could even feel a spaghetti-thin thread of the stuff worming its way down the hole at the end of his dick. Its passage inside his urethra was coarse and painful, and he screamed his muffled screams against a throat full of shit. The invading entity ignored Farid's yowls and continued to snake its way inside his body, whereupon it sprouted yet more razor claws, which tore at him from the inside, as if eager to meet with their compatriots that were digging and digesting him through from the outside.

Farid's body soon grew limp as the air stilled in his lungs, and his ruined body bled out. The last thing he saw before his eyes dissolved and collapsed into their own viscous slime were floating sweet corn kernels and what appeared to be slivers of tomato skins.

The body of Claire's shit held its victim upright, and to Hayley and Garcia, it looked as if Farid and the entity were locked in an intimate slow dance at the end of Prom. It held on to Farid tightly and pulled his suppurating remains into its own shifting body. It ripped, clawed and absorbed him. Even the hardness of Farid's bones succumbed to the enzymes and digestive juices of Claire Jepson's excrement, and they fizzled and crumbled into nothing.

And then he was gone.

The huge, brown shape at the boardroom's only door pulsed, undulated and glistened, and now it looked taller, more human in form.

Hayley and Garcia could only watch with their mouths agape. The shape slithered across the natural slate floor towards them, and they felt glued to their seats, unable to flee, even when faced with what had just happened to their Vice President.

Finally, as the stinking thing was close enough to reach her with an exploratory tendril, Hayley found her motivation.

"Get off of me, you fucking piece of shit!" she screamed.

"Now, that's just plain offensive," the shit said.

Hayley could see a dripping, gaping maw open and close in what passed for the thing's face as the words took shape. And were those *teeth*? "There really is no reason to be like that, Hayley."

Hayley jumped out of her chair and leapt over Garcia, who was paralyzed by his own fear-freeze and way beyond any help that she was prepared to provide him; *every man, woman and child for themselves*!

She skirted around the meeting table, happy to have that reassuring lump of solid wood between her and the heap of crap that slipped by the catatonic Garcia, as if he weren't there. One eye on the door—her escape—and Hayley darted around the room with an agility she never knew she had.

The excrement launched itself across the table and left a formidable skid of lumpy brown-green slime in its wake.

It thrust out a dozen or so of its snake-like arms, three of which wrapped around a chunky ankle and brought Hayley down like a bear in a trap.

Hayley screamed and kicked as the thing loomed, a rancorous and oozing brown, over her.

"Help me, Edson!" she cried out. "Pleeeeese!" Her voice cracked and she struggled against the grip on her ankle that was so tight that it was cutting off the circulation to her foot.

Edson Garcia didn't acknowledge her. He sat in his spot passively, his eyes staring but seeing nothing, as if simply awaiting his own fate.

"I'll do anything! Please, don't..." Hayley's words gagged in her throat as a fresh wave of putrescent odor assaulted her nose. She lay, supine with her back pressed against the wall, staring up at the human-esque column of feces that was standing over her.

"Anything?" the voice teased. Again—*teeth*? "You really ought to be careful with that one, Hayley." And Hayley thought she caught sound of the lightest of laughs and fancied that she saw the thing smile.

And that she found the smile hauntingly familiar.

"Farid?" Hayley murmured.

A tendril of considerable girth shot out from the middle of the shit-thing. It thickened and took on a firm shape, as its end disappeared up Hayley's hitched-up, sensible skirt. She let out a shrill ululation, as she saw that there was an unmistakable phallic shape of the end of the tendril. Shit, the thing even had a lustrous, pink glans.

The thick phallus gave a mighty thrust at Haley's cunt and buried itself inside her, and she gasped; the thing was surprisingly hard. Instead of fucking her around the side of her panties, or ripping them from her, the tendril pushed the rough material up deep into her vagina and created a tight wedgie that bit into her asshole in a not entirely unpleasant way.

"Oh!" Hayley exclaimed.

Unable to move, skewered, as she was by an enormous shit-dick, Hayley dug her fingernails into the hard floor and pressed her back into the wall behind her, as if by doing so she could push herself through it and on to freedom.

The seeping shape towered over Hayley and began a forceful, rhythmic thrust that pumped away at her pussy like some steam-driven machine from the Industrial Revolution. Hayley, for her part, spread her chunky thighs as wide as they could go and bore down on the second thickest thing she'd ever had inside her vag' (the first on the list was the time she and a guy she'd picked up in a bar had fooled around with the baseball bat she kept under the bed in case of intruders).

And then Hayley came. She came vigorously and screamed it out against the palm of her hand, biting down on the soft flesh to stifle her embarrassment. Spent, she looked up at the shifting mountain of filth and saw the dripping, gaping maw open once more, as if it were happy to have provided Hayley Barnett, CFO of Jepson Software Solutions, with her last orgasm.

And this time, she *did* see the teeth.

From the end of the fat tendril buried deep inside Hayley's vagina, there erupted a razor-sharp claw. The tendril then grew longer and snaked up into her body, hacking a path through her viscera. Before Hayley had time to register the keen pang of pain in her internals, the claw had sliced up through her cervix, out through her womb, and was making its way through the tight coils of her intestines.

When it reached her heart, Hayley felt the hot, sharp stab as the claw punctured the beating muscle and a thick, pumping flood of liberated blood filled the inside of her chest and deluged her lungs.

Too late, Hayley tried to move away from the assault on her body; all she was able to achieve was a feeble slide to her left and a sad, choking sound that gurgled from her throat.

One last thrust from the excrement and the claw tore its way out through Hayley's eye socket. It popped her eye out from its home on the way out, and the bloodied orb dangled against her cheek by its optic nerve and the one remaining muscle that had not been sliced through. And through her hanging eye—the blue one—Hayley could see down between her legs and the ever-widening phallus of the shit-being as is continued to disappear up into her cunt.

The dick increased its girth until Hayley Barnett's slumped, lifeless body split open, and her innards spilled out in a mixture of ruined flesh and amorphous slime, as she continued to be digested from the insides out.

Garcia finally came to his senses, and self-preservation kicked in, albeit far too late. He struggled to his feet and darted for the door. Three steps and his feet slid from under him; the disgusting mix of feces and dissolving people had rendered the floor traction-less. He hit the ground with a solid *WHUMPH!* that knocked the air from his lungs and sent shards of pain jarring along his spine. And try as he may to get to his feet, Farid's legs just slipped and slid in the mess, and he looked like a dog chasing rabbits in its sleep.

And then, the stinking, murderous bulk of excrement was upon him.

***

Claire Jepson surveyed her boardroom. It was one almighty, disgusting mess; a veritable shitstorm of stinking, slimy gloop and drying globs of brown crap that covered the floor, the walls, and even some parts of the grey-flecked ceiling tiles.

"What the heck happened in here?" Ethan Foote, her Security Manager asked. "That really is one bad smell, Ma'am." He held a lilac handkerchief over his nose, a surprisingly feminine object for such a mountain of a man.

"It looks to me like a sewer pipe burst. What would you say, Mr. Foote?" Claire strained her neck to look up at the guy. He towered over her at six feet six—possibly seven and was easily as broad as two men. He had hard, toned muscles that rippled beneath the thin cotton-mix uniform shirt and a chiseled, almost Neanderthal face that one could only describe as *primitive*.

He was also the only person in her company—quite possibly in her entire world now that Karl's deception had come to light—that Claire knew she could trust implicitly. They had a history that dated back to early sexual explorations in high school, and although Ethan was your archetypal meat-head quarterback type who was nowhere near the shiniest button on the shirt, they had remained good friends in the years since graduation. Sure, he was married now, and had five snot-nosed brats with the flat-chested, nerdy-looking girl who'd been Debate Club Captain (who'd have *thought*?!) but the guy was still good for a booty call whenever Claire had some time—or a hole (*or two*)—to fill.

He was also damned good at his job, being loyal, fearless and incredibly protective of Claire.

"Sewer pipe," Foote repeated. "Burst. Yes, Ma'am."

"I'm lucky I stepped out for a few minutes to grab the notes I'd left in my office—on my desk," Claire spoke slowly, deliberately. He may have had the longest, most skilled tongue she'd ever had the privilege to have lapping at her cunt (and with all the enthusiasm of a cat who'd gotten the most expensive of creams), and the most magnificent cock to have ever penetrated her, but Ethan Foote didn't catch on to a hint so quick.

"Lucky, yeah," he grunted. "Say, where'd the others go?"

"Home to change." Claire laughed. "Wouldn't you?"

"Yes, Ma'am." Foote grinned as he peered around the shit-stained boardroom. "I guess I would."

Claire patted her security guard/casual fuck-friend on his rock-solid bicep and made her excuses. She told him that she had to leave for a meeting now, and would he mind *awfully* getting some people in to clean this unholy mess up?

"Of course, Ma'am." Foote smiled at her like the kid who just got picked to be hall monitor. "You can leave everything to me." And Claire knew that he would be watching her butt sway as she retreated down the hallway, and she felt a twinge in her pussy as she wondered when he'd next be balls deep inside it.

Claire walked quickly and with purpose towards the main doors of her office building; it was a walk that screamed *don't even try talking to me!,* and her employees scurried out of her way with barely a nod or a good morning.

Out through the double glass doors and into the welcome and incredibly refreshing outdoor air, Claire gulped in deep lungs full of the stuff like a drowning man resurfaced, eager to be rid of the fecal stink that clung to the inside of her nostrils and mouth like a viscous coating.

On her way across the dark asphalt of her parking lot, Claire passed by a bland looking guy who she guessed was most likely trying to hawk insurance or photocopiers, judging him by his drab, grey suit and sad, weary eyes. The man was on his way towards her office building, and he tried to make eye contact and smile.

Claire just blanked him—so not in the mood.

Ordinarily, she would have stopped and taken the time to rip the guy a new one. Her absolute number one pet hate in business were salespeople who dropped in on spec and expected her—or her incredibly well-paid staff—to drop everything and listen to their desperate sales pitch. It was most infuriating.

But not today.

Today was turning into one of those *difficult* days, so she decided to let Ethan deal with the man. All Claire wanted to do was go home, take another long, hot shower, and sooth her jangled nerves with expensive single malt on ice and by stroking her cat. She shook her head in a failed attempt to clear it. Just when she was beginning to convince herself that she had hallucinated the whole motel incident, whatever had happened there had happened in her boardroom, and here she was again, doubting her own sanity.

Sure, she'd not actually been witness to any more speaking bodily wastes, but there could be no doubting what had occurred during her absence from the boardroom. She'd seen what her crap-thing had done to Karl and his skinny bitch, and Claire didn't have to stretch her imagination too far to guess at the likely fate of her board members.

Either that or this had been one bitch of a coincidence. Hadn't she heard someone once say that there was no such thing as coincidence? Yeah, it was either Sherlock Holmes or that smartass on NCIS, damned if her befuddled brain could remember which one.

Striding across the meticulously lined parking lot to

her awaiting Range Rover, Claire Jepson made herself a mental note; take time out sometime soon to buy a goddamned cat.

FOUR

At precisely the same time as Edson Garcia was smothering to death under a preternatural volume of animated excrement, Tony Wyatt was picking the lock of Claire Jepson's kitchen door.

"You learned a new trick." Krystal had a modicum of admiration in her voice for her husband.

"Yep, I taught myself especially for this occasion." Tony Wyatt smiled at his wife and peered down the ink-black crack of her cleavage. "It's amazing what they post on YouTube these days."

"Can you hurry it up, Tony?" Samuel was his usual, antsy self, which made Krystal wonder once more why he ever agreed to join in on their nefarious adventures, considering how fucking nervous he got; she'd never seen a man sweat so much in her life. *Maybe that was his thing*, she hypothesized, *perhaps Samuel got off on being shit-scared of his own fucking shadow.*

"Calm down, Sammy," Krystal placated. "It's not like the neighbors are going to see us now, is it?"

She gave an exaggerated look around.

There were no neighbors to see, it was quite as simple as that. Claire Jepson's rambling, red brick, two-storey house nestled in the center of four acres of exquisitely manicured grounds that were dotted with mature oaks. The nearest neighbor was at the very least a mile away, and Krystal reckoned that the three of them could do their breaking and entering bare-assed naked if they chose to, and no one would see. But then again, where would be the fun in that?

They had still taken no chances, though. Krystal had directed Tony to park a half-mile away at a popular beauty spot, where their bland SUV had blended in nicely with those of the day-hikers and sightseers. They had walked the rest of the way to the Jepson house with Samuel complaining about his feet most of the way.

There was a gentle click.

"There!" Tony exclaimed, almost as surprised with his success at lock picking as his wife and his fuckbuddy were. It should really have been less of a surprise, what with his aptitude with a scalpel and a beating heart, but, nonetheless, Tony was suitably smug.

The door swung open, and they all stepped in. Tony made sure to lock the door after himself; the last thing they needed was to spook Jepson with an unlocked door when she came home and spoil any surprises.

"What *is* that smell?" Krystal crinkled her nose at the faint aroma of bad drains that hung in the air. It was a smell she'd associate more with an addict's trailer—and she'd seen plenty of *those* on her adventures with Tony and Samuel—than a ten thousand square foot luxury home

"I'm not smelling anything," her husband replied and inhaled deeply through his nose to make his point.

"Doesn't surprise me." Krystal spat. Much of Tony's formative years had been spent with a rolled twenty stuck up his nose, so much so that doctors had told him that the cocaine had eroded his septum to the thickness of tissue paper. You could pretty much drop a deuce on the man's top lip, and he'd not be able to smell it.

"Smells like shit," Samuel said with his customary finesse. "Reminds me of the time I got Salmonella off of my kid sister's red-eared slider. Hated that slimy little bastard."

"The kid or the turtle?" Tony asked.

"Yeah." Samuel grimaced and set off towards the stairs.

The house dripped luxury, from the expensive deep-shag carpets to the polished wood detail on the walls to the exquisite, handmade designer furniture. And, whilst Krystal preferred her own loft apartment home in the fashionable part of town—this was just a little too ostentatious for her city tastes—she was forced to admit to just a soupcon of envy; this place really was something else.

There was a plasma TV the size of a small multiplex screen that took up most of one of the lounge walls. It was faced by a cream colored, soft leather couch that Krystal just couldn't resist sinking her butt into.

"Oh, wow," she moaned, as she sank deep into the couch, and it enveloped her ass and bare thighs with soft calf skin. "This is what couches in heaven must feel like." She stroked it as one would a fluffy pet and leaned her head back.

Tony planted himself next to her, so close that their thighs touched. He sighed as he too sank into the couch's extravagance. "We *really* ought to get ourselves one of these, my darling." He said and slid a hand the short distance up his wife's skirt.

"Oh, yes, please, lover," Krystal purred.

"What do you say, Samuel?"

But Samuel was no longer in the living room. He'd gone exploring.

***

Samuel Nester crept quietly along the upstairs hallway. He was not exactly sure why he was creeping around, since he knew for a fact that there was no one home. Even so, it seemed like the appropriate thing to do under the circumstances, like talking quietly in an empty church.

He peeked through a couple of doors. Some were conveniently open; a couple he had to crack open himself. One thing was for certain, this lady had a lot of spare bedrooms, and each one was made up like the place was a show home. Perhaps she had a lot of guests or, as Samuel preferred to imagine, plenty of hot, rampant orgies in which she indulged herself with every pleasure of the flesh one could imagine.

And Samuel Nester could imagine one hell of a lot of those.

Before long, his prying was rewarded, and he found exactly what he was looking for: the master bedroom. He let himself in and quietly closed the heavy door behind him.

Claire's boudoir, in contrast to the cheesy chintz of the guest rooms, was actually quite sparse. It had institutional white walls and was dominated by a four-poster bed way beyond King-sized. The bed was laid with crisp, white sheets, a half dozen of the world's whitest, fluffiest pillows, and a thick, white woolen quilt. There was an antique, multi-drawered nightstand—most likely English oak—a white, velvet sofa, and matching chaise-lounge and that was it. No TV, no static bike, no computer, in fact, nothing that Samuel would have pictured in a millionaire's bedroom.

Quite disappointing, really.

He pushed open the door to the spacious ensuite bathroom and caught a whiff of the smell that had obviously drifted from here to downstairs but paid it no mind, he'd found what he'd come looking for.

Samuel rifled through the wicker laundry basket that snuggled between the Jacuzzi bath and the bidet and fished out a pair of black panties. He rubbed the undergarment between his thumb and forefinger to determine if they were of just the right silkiness for his liking.

Indeed, they were.

He turned Claire's used panties around in his hand to delight in the slick, cool feel of the material and the thin white crust that streaked the gusset. Samuel lifted the panties to his nose, inhaled deeply, and the dank, musk scent of pussy caused the blood to rush to his dick like a tsunami of Biblical proportions.

With due reverence, Samuel placed the panties on the toilet seat, returned to the bedroom and rummaged through the nightstand. He only had to open two of the six drawers before he found what he just *knew* would be there: Claire's sex toy collection. He grunted as he fished through—and sniffed some of—the assortment of vibrators, cock-shaped dildos, nipple clamps and butt plugs. Of course, she'd have sex toys in the nightstand, why did these people have to be so fucking predictable?

Also, Samuel just knew that there would be a tube of *Astroglide* in with the toys—there always was. He grabbed it and returned to the bathroom and the panties.

Samuel pulled off his shirt and dropped his jeans and underwear to his ankles. He pressed the lavatory handle and settled himself down on to the seat. He'd made sure to lift the lid first; as he much preferred to have his balls dangle free rather than be squashed beneath his buttocks while he jerked off. Upon lifting the lid, Samuel noticed the whiff was a little stronger there, the streaks of brown along the porcelain not in the least bit faded. It was as if the toilet had been used not so long ago, which was strange; their brief had specifically stated that Jepson had been away overnight and would go directly to her office. No matter, the scent made him feel covert and dirty; and that enhanced the turn-on.

He shrugged, popped the lube lid, and squirted a generous blob of clear jelly onto the inside of the panties. Then he wrapped the silky material tight around his painfully hard penis.

"Ahhhh," he sighed. That felt so damn good. So much so that when he espied a used tampon in the bin by his foot, he only considered it for a second or two, preferring instead to concentrate on the slick underwear.

Samuel slid the panties along the shaft of his penis and twirled them over the sensitive skin of its head. The sensation from the silky material and the warm wetness of the lubricant were almost too much to bear, especially so since he'd not long since had his dick buried to the hilt in Krystal Wyatt's delectable pussy. But, he persevered, and was rewarded by an orgasmic tingle that spread from his cock, down into his tightening balls and up into the pit of his stomach.

Increased strokes now, Samuel made sure that every inch of his greasy dick felt the benefit of Claire Jepson's cunt-soiled underpants. He felt his come pooling in his prostate, ripe and ready to spurt. This was going to be one doozy of a jerk-off, he could feel it. And all thanks to the illicitness of breaking in someone else's home, masturbating with their used panties, and sitting in the stink of their most recent defecation.

Which, now it was back in his mind, Samuel was sure had grown more pungent as he had gone about his self-love.

Without breaking his rhythm, Samuel peered down between his legs, past his dick and into the toilet bowl.

Funny, he thought, *could have sworn I'd flushed that.*

The water in the toilet bowl had turned a thin, brackish shade of light brown, although as Samuel watched, it did seem to be getting a trifle darker. It began to bubble like a miniature hot mud spring, and the rank, sulfurous stink that emanated from it made Samuel gag. Nonetheless undeterred, he kept on pumping at that magnificent cock of his, so close to orgasm that he couldn't have stopped even if he'd wanted to. A guttural grunt, an involuntary jerk of the hips accompanied by another grunt, and Samuel shot his jizz into Claire's Victoria's Secrets.

As Samuel's dick twitched for the final spurt of his ejaculation, the thick, brown water in the toilet bowl shot upwards in a thumb-thick stream as precise and straight as a laser beam.

Samuel's back stiffened, ramrod straight, as the reeking stream shot directly into his anus and up into the colon beyond. He tried to move away, but the shock of the intrusion into his body along with the rapidly increasing volume of the liquid held him fast as if he were glued down. Samuel could do nothing more than clutch at either side of the ceramic seat with clawed hands with the black silk panties glued to his dick by his own spendings while the monstrous stream filled him up.

The pain as his colon ruptured was the worst he'd ever experienced in his life—even more so than the outrageously large kidney stone he'd passed the pervious Easter. It felt to Samuel as if someone was inside of him, ripping at his guts with jagged fingernails; a sick, tearing sensation that spread liquid fire through his body. His small intestines went next. Fat and bloated by the voluminous stream of liquid shit that flooded them, they split in innumerable places along their eighteen-foot length, spilling out digestive acids and stuffing his body cavity with their putrid mess.

Samuel sat transfixed by the agonies that were being inflicted on his insides. His mouth opened and closed as if he were screaming, but no sound save a thin whistle of air managed to escape him.

Next, the fecal matter filled his stomach, and Samuel watched it distend his belly 'till it looked as though he were nine months into gestation and ready to drop quadruplets. Then came the inevitable *POP!* as his cardiac sphincter tore open; a sound so strident, that Samuel was convinced Krystal and Tony must have heard it from downstairs.

Liquid shit poured out of Samuel's mouth and nose, no longer held back by the tight muscles of his stomach. He'd felt his stomach rupture and a hot, full sensation had washed through him. Sadly for Samuel, the thick flood of stinking matter that poured from his face was nowhere near enough to alleviate the growing pressure inside his body, and before long, he was reduced to a fat, bloated blimp perched upon the lavatory, like Humpty in the nursery rhyme on his wall.

One final, silent scream before the mercy of death, and Samuel's flesh ripped apart under the sheer volume of liquid that was being forced into it. The rents opened up along his right flank and across his belly and made cruel, grinning mouths in his flesh that spat scarlet arcs of blood, lumpy brown feces, and chunks of wrecked, dissolving innards far and wide across the bathroom.

Then as quickly as it had begun, the vicious jet

from below ceased. Samuel slumped downwards, and his ruined body collapsed into the toilet like some macabre moonwalk, deflating at the end of a kiddie's party.

The stinking liquid slithered back towards the toilet bowl, dragging with it Samuel's spilled fluids and dissolving chunks of flesh. Slowly but surely, it began to clear the bathroom as the water inside the toilet bowl bubbled and churned and went about the business of dissolving what remained of Samuel Nester and sucking his residue down into the sewers.

***

"Where the fuck is he?" Krystal grumbled. She shifted her sweaty, bare backside on the couch, and it made the leather creak. "He's always wandering off to masturbate; he'll wear his dick down to the fucking bone if he's not careful." Of course, she knew full well that the human penis does not contain ossification of any kind, but it was still a good and most apt phrase.

"Never mind Samuel, what about *this*?" Tony whined. He was standing in front of his wife, dick rigid and pointing directly into her face.

"I am *not* putting that thing in my mouth after you had it in that theater skank." Krystal was firm. "And certainly not before you get some antibiotics inside you."

"But I'm not back at the hospital 'till tomorrow morning." More whining.

It was times like this that Krystal was pleased that she had two men in her life; it was not often that they'd both be in a whiney mood at the same time.

Tony had not even had the decency nor taken the time to rinse his cock off under the faucet, and it stunk pretty bad, especially as close as he had it to Krystal's nose. She eyed it with distaste, as one would a particularly gross exhibit at a museum of medical curiosities. She could see for herself that her husband's typically proudworthy member still displayed the residuals of Meth-Whore's partially dried, green-streaked pussy slime along its flanks. There were also a couple of rust-red scab flakes that clung in his pubic hair like oversized crab lice. And she'd bet a month's salary that there'd be some regular sized, real ones of those somewhere in there, too.

"But I pleasured you, my love," Tony persisted and wiggled his dick in her direction, not realizing just how much he was *really* getting on her nerves now. "It's only fair."

Krystal snorted her derision. As if Tony's frantic fingering of her clit ever added weight to any of Tony's arguments. She'd genuinely lost count of the times she'd relieved her husband's priapic dick in her hand, on her tits, between her toes, and in her face and gotten nothing back because he was too drunk, too busy, or just too damned lazy to make the effort.

Granted, he was good with his fingers when he *did* make the effort, and he had just given her three—no, four—intense orgasms that had made her toes tingle and created a stain on Claire Jepson's couch that Krystal thought looked to be in the shape of Bob Hope, but she'd not be touching Tony's disgusting, stinky thing right now for all the tea in china.

"We should go find Samuel." Krystal slid sideways and stood up, putting an end to Tony's hopes once and for all. She glanced downwards from his disappointed face and saw to her relief that his cock was already beginning to subside. She saw, also, that some of the glistening snail-trail she'd made on the expensive couch was still wet. Krystal bent over and rubbed it in with the heel of her hand to get rid of it, not really sure why she was bothering, given the circumstances.

Krystal headed towards the stairs, straightening her skirt as she walked, so that it at least covered the crack between her buttocks. It was nice for a change, to have had an orgasm or two (four!), and not have had to deal with the fallout of sticky sperm from between her thighs.

Tony followed his wife with the rejected look still etched on his face. As he walked, he stuffed his dick back into his pants, zipped up, then sniffed at his fingers with disdain. His nose turned up at the putrid stink, and he wiped the offending digits on the seat of his jeans.

"Samuel?" Krystal called out. "Are you up here?"

Silence.

"Maybe he's busy?" Tony offered.

"Oh, I have no doubt at all that he'll be busy," Krystal growled. "He needs to learn a little more self-restraint and focus when we're working. I mean, how would it be if he disappeared from one of his high-level finance meetings to choke his fucking chicken every chance he got?"

Tony cracked a grin. "Actually, I heard…"

"It's just not acceptable!" Krystal barked.

"But, you just had me finger-bang you downstairs." Tony was genuinely puzzled.

"Tony," Krystal stopped and looked him straight in the eye, "I'm a woman—I can multitask." She patted his cheek and headed into Claire Jepson's bedroom, where she recoiled at the smell that wafted out to greet her. "Hmm, I thought we'd find Samuel in here." She looked around and spotted the nightstand drawer that yawned open. "Looks like he's been up to his old tricks again." She rummaged through Claire Jepson's impressive selection of sex toys and accessories. Krystal allowed her fingers to linger over a small, purple rubber whip and a pair of vicious-looking nipple clamps with black rubber pincers. "Dirty bastard."

"You in the bathroom, Samuel?" Tony shouted, too lazy to actually go look. He was met with yet more silence.

"I guess he's not," Krystal said. "Otherwise, he'd be inviting us in to join in him with whatever it is that he's doing with his dick." She could feel her temper rising and thought of the thermometers they used in cartoons where the character's anger was portrayed by the climbing red liquid until it burst out of the top like a geyser.

"So where is he?"

"My guess," Krystal sounded downright mean now. "would be that he snuck out the back door while you were flicking my fucking peanut." She snarled the expletive with true venom.

And that would make it Take Two of *Samuel Nester Bails Mid-Job*.

The last time he'd done it to them had been when they were paid handsomely to beat the living shit out of some lowlife who'd stolen a cache of drugs from another lowlife who fancied himself as the local Scarface. The rub had been that Krystal, Tony and Samuel were to be paid an additional bonus of one-thousand dollars between them for each of Lowlife #1's teeth they brought back from the beating. Samuel had been happy with providing the fists and feet that had ultimately helped keep the guy in ICU for six weeks, but had wussed out and gotten all squeamish when it came to pulling the teeth. He'd made some lame excuse about him not being a doctor and that *they* were used to such things and had just left the Wyatts to it.

By means of making things even, Krystal and Tony had kept the entire thirty-two-thousand-dollar bonus to themselves, and Samuel had none of the chutzpah to dare say a damned thing about it.

"Looks like we're on our own again, lover." Krystal shrugged her shoulders and wandered over to the bathroom door.

She still had to satisfy her own curiosity that Samuel was not simply hiding from them or so wrapped up in some masturbatory scene so elaborate that he just hadn't heard them calling. And besides, she wanted to have a gawk at Rich Lady's bathroom.

"Did you hear that?" Tony's voice was suddenly a whisper.

Krystal stood rooted to the spot, her hand on the ensuite doorknob. She cocked her head, dog-like, to listen.

More noise.

From downstairs.

The front door slammed shut and was followed by the rattle of keys on the hall tree. Then the clatter of heels on the Italian tiled floor.

"Fuck!" Krystal exclaimed in a loud whisper. "She's not supposed to be due home for at least another four hours!"

Tony looked petrified, and the color drained from his face as surely as if someone had pulled the plug that held in all of his blood. His eyes darted to the bed, to the gap under it.

Krystal nodded and hurried over, the bathroom door and Samuel already forgotten.

Tony scrabbled under the bed and wriggled his body in to the center—the least visible position. Krystal made ready to join him when she saw that the nightstand drawer was still open, and she froze.

"Hurry!" Tony stage whispered.

"Give me a second!"

The sound of footsteps heading up the stairs resounded heavily in Krystal's guilty ears, like Poe's telltale heart under the floorboards. She knew that she couldn't leave the sex toy drawer open because a woman with such obvious OCD as Claire Jepson would die before she ever left a drawer open. Therefore, she would know that someone had been—or still was—in her home. Everything in its place, a place for everything, as Krystal's equally obsessive Grandmother would say.

One look at the drawer that *should* be shut tight, and Jepson could panic and be calling the police, and that would be that.

All over.

Krystal stepped over and pushed the drawer shut, cringing at the grating noise it made as wood slid against wood. She was convinced that the owner of the approaching footsteps would hear the sound and well, that really *would* be that.

Then, by the unearthly power that is Murphy's Law, the drawer jammed on one of the nipple clamps.

"Shit!" Krystal hissed as she tried to force the rubber-coated pincer end of the clamp back into the sex-drawer.

It was wedged tight.

The footsteps grew louder, now coming from the hallway and towards the bedroom.

Krystal pulled on the drawer and gave the errant nipple clamp a hard shove that split one of her French-manicured nails to the quick, and she saw in her peripheral vision the bedroom door handle begin to turn.

FIVE

Claire bustled into her bedroom and stopped dead in her tracks. There was something wrong, something that alerted her sixth sense.

She looked around but could see nothing immediately amiss. Everything was as she'd left it earlier that morning, when she'd rushed in clutching her stomach and vacated her body swiftly and efficiently from both ends into the toilet.

"You're getting paranoid, old girl," she chastised herself and took great comfort in breaking the lonely silence that blanketed her house.

Hardly surprising I'm paranoid, Claire thought to herself. It had been a thoroughly bizarre day after all, one which she was still attempting to process. And then there was the ever-present scent of stale poop that still emanated from the bathroom and seemed to be hanging around her like some sort of forlorn ghost.

Claire walked over to her ensuite door and paused with her hand on the handle. Again, she sensed that something was not quite right. Something seemed a little skewed in her usually regimented reality.

Was it the smell? Her mind raced with myriad images of Karl and the motel room, of weird, talking things that had no business having a voice. And then over to the stinking mess in her boardroom and her strangely absent Board.

All the while, a little voice (mercifully not the one with a British accent) was telling her not to open the door; *for God's sakes, don't open that door!*

Claire threw open the bathroom door and kicked off her shoes. She peeled off her skirt and shirt, brassiere and panties, and hurled the lot from a distance, one by one, into her laundry basket.

"Yeah!" she cheered herself as each article of her clothing hit home.

From beneath Claire's bed, Krystal and Tony watched and bided their time. They both enjoyed the impromptu strip show-cum basketball display and reveled in the titillating spectacle of their quarry's naked, vulnerable tits, ass and pussy as she went about her ablutions.

Claire padded barefoot over to the shower, flicked it on, and an instant stream of steaming water thundered out from the wide, brass shower head.

She flipped up the toilet lid and lowered herself onto the chilly seat. Claire glanced down at the tainted water in the bowl, saw that she'd left a handful of floaters (*little presents*, her Granny used to call them in that quaint *grandparenty* way of hers—Christmas must have been a real hoot when Granny was a kid!) during her unscheduled visit that morning. Oddly, the pungent odor from the bowl seemed disproportionately stronger than the 'presents' suggested; it smelled like something had died down there.

"Could have sworn I'd flushed you little fuckers away," she said, the irony of the one-sided conversation not lost on her. "Your days are numbered, ha ha ha." She made with her best evil-Nazi laugh, and that made her smile a tad.

Normally, a lingering lavatory aroma wouldn't have bothered Claire all that much. She had quite gotten used to the theme and odor of her day, and she was one of the few women she knew of who were comfortable in the presence of her own excretory smells. As with most guys, Claire could happily remain seated on the toilet until she'd finished her Wall Street Journal or Cosmo article, comfortable enough to sit in her own stink, unflushed and unwiped.

But today, she'd had enough of errant fecal matter, and she made the executive decision that she would much rather pee in the shower and banish these unpleasant relics of her day to the sewers before *they* started answering her back.

Claire flushed and watched as the tiny brown spheres bobbed and danced around in the churning water before hurrying away down the U-bend as if they were late for something.

She stepped into the warm, inviting shower, and the water was pre-programmed to be just as she liked it—slightly on the too-hot side, so that it stung her skin like a thousand annoyed wasps. Claire shampooed her hair and scrubbed every inch of her skin until it felt raw and cleansed; would she ever be rid of that smell?

As Claire fell under the spell of the warm, humid cocoon of the shower cubicle and the fierce jets of steaming water, a twinge in her bloated bladder reminded her that she had promised it a shower-micturate in lieu of letting loose on the soiled toilet, and she was only too happy to oblige.

The gush of pee that flooded the inside of Claire's

thigh and down along the muscular shape of her leg felt warmer even than the shower water, although she knew that to be impossible. Nonetheless, she sighed at the delightful, twinned sensations of her bladder's thankful release and the soothing deluge of the resulting bodily fluid on her tingling skin.

"Shower's over, lady." A gruff voice startled her.

"Yeah, get the fuck out, bitch." Another voice; this one female.

Claire glanced through the frosted shower door and saw that there were two blurred outlines in her bathroom. She thought for a second or two that her fecal monster had returned and had brought along a girlfriend.

The shower door flung open, and Claire saw two very human shapes. She opened her mouth and let out a piercing scream, flailing her arms at the hands that reached in to grab her.

Krystal dragged Claire from the shower and found it a struggle to keep a grip on her quarry's wet, slippery skin. She gave a well-aimed punch to Claire's screaming mouth, which shut the complaining bitch up rather effectively.

Claire was stunned by the punch, more though of the shock of unexpected violence against her person than the pain. The punch made glittering stars spiral behind her eyes and gave her the metallic tang of blood in her mouth. She was aware, also, that she was still voiding her bladder.

"She's peeing," the man said.

"I can see that." The woman's voice was deep and husky.

Claire saw the woman look down at the rivulet of pee that trickled down her leg to soak into the white, fluffy shower mat to stain it pale yellow. And she saw an unmistakably familiar glint flittering in the woman's eye; like this was the horniest thing she'd ever seen.

Seizing the chance of Krystal's temporary distraction, Claire wriggled free of her grasp. She gave the woman a hard shove in the chest and felt her hand sink deep into soft, liquid breast. The woman gave a startled cry and staggered backwards. Next, Claire felled the skinny guy, who was just standing there with a vacant expression on his face. She aimed a swift, hard kick to his balls. Wishful thinking or did she just feel something go *pop*?

Tony gripped his crotch with both hands and sank to his knees. Thus, he was unable to prevent the naked and dripping wet Claire from dodging by him on her way to the door.

"You'd best stop right there, bitch," Krystal's voice dripped with menace, "before I blow your fucking tits off."

Claire spun around and found herself staring down the barrel of a snub-nosed revolver, not entirely dissimilar to her own. The woman aimed it directly at Claire's face, and the unblinking eye of its muzzle dared her to make that next move.

"I didn't know you'd brought a gun, Krystal," Tony wheezed, his breath strained and his voice an octave and a half higher than usual.

"What did you expect, Tony?" Krystal didn't bother to disguise her contempt. "That we'd just ask nicely if she wouldn't mind cooperating with us?"

Tony shrugged and got back on his feet, cradling his aching balls with one hand.

"A-are you going to shoot me?" Claire asked, her eyes still fixed on the gun.

"Not if you do as you're told, like a good little girl," Krystal said, and her eyes scanned the length and breadth of Claire Jepson's exposed body to take in her soap-slicked tits, firm, dripping belly, and the burst of fluffy black down between her milky thighs.

Claire felt uncomfortable under the woman's stare. Naked, vulnerable. "Could I please get dressed?" Her voice was soft, passive.

"And have you rooting around in your closet for your own gun?" Krystal snapped. "And don't insult my intelligence by trying to tell me a rich bitch like you living all alone doesn't own a firearm."

"I wasn't going to." Claire offered a placatory smile. "May I at least have a towel, then?" She held out her arms in a submissive gesture, emphasizing that she was dripping wet and starting to get cold. Gooseflesh prickled her arms, thighs and belly.

"You can fucking drip dry," Krystal informed her. "Now get your fucking ass downstairs." She wiggled the gun at Claire to underline the command.

Claire could see that she had no choice but to comply, remain as non-threatening as was possible, and wait for the right chance to escape. Whilst she didn't know yet what her home invaders wanted; she was sure that they didn't mean to kill her. If they'd wanted that, Claire Jepson knew that she'd be dead already.

So, she was worth something to them alive. To Claire, that meant an opportunity to talk to, reason perhaps, or maybe even overpower them. If she could just get a hold of the gun—presuming they only had the one between them, and there were no other accomplices in the house—then the balance of power would shift pretty fucking quickly. Claire also took comfort in the fact that the two—*Tony* and *Kristin*, was it?—were intimidated enough to keep her naked in their pathetic *High School Psychology 101* attempt to maintain an advantage.

What they clearly hadn't factored in to their plan was that Tony was male. And in the presence of a nude—and not entirely unattractive—female, all bets were off.

"Okay, move it!" Krystal ushered Claire from the bathroom, impatient as if reading her captive's thoughts.

Tony took a moment to switch off the shower—ever the thrifty one, was Tony Wyatt—and shuffle out behind his wife and the naked millionaire chick.

He closed the ensuite door as he left, and behind him the water in the toilet bowl began to gurgle and bubble, like the mud in an exotic hot spring.

SIX

"This is *another* message for Hayley," Krystal snarled into her cell phone. She paced back and forth at the farthest point in the room away from Claire, whom she had instructed to remain seated on the couch and not *fucking* move. More precisely, she had entrusted Tony with the gun and instructed him to make sure their captive didn't move. *If she tries to stand up, shoot her in the fucking tits,* is what she'd told her husband.

Even Tony couldn't fuck that up.

Claire sat quietly on the cool leather couch, and her damp—but—drying skin was sticking to it. She felt uncomfortable and understandably exposed, and the pee on her leg had dried now, and its pungent, alkaline aroma prickled her nose. It was, she found, not an entirely unpleasant alternative to the poop smell, and it made her feel strangely—*unfaithful*?

While she sat with her legs crossed, like a proper lady, Claire made no attempt to hide the twin mounds of her breasts. Her nipples were not aroused right now and lay soft and smooth against the line of her breasts, topping each one like pink snow on fleshy mountain tops.

Claire concentrated hard on suppressing the panic that raged inside her. She knew all too well that if she was to survive this ordeal, she had to remain calm, and she also had it figured that if she could create a little friction between her captors, she may just be able to create a chance of escape.

It was obvious that her two kidnappers were married, not only from the matching wedding bands, which were of a distinctive Celtic weave pattern, but by the way they interacted with each other, namely, the woman treated the guy like crap, and he just took it. And what better way to create friction between a married couple than with the ol' green-eyed monster?

Being as completely *au naturel* as she was, Claire was delightfully aware of the power her body had over the lecherous Tony. So, she uncrossed and crossed her legs at opportune moments to flash him a hint of her pussy and its gently protruding inner labia. To add to the allure, she made a show of stroking her breasts, under the pretence of feeling cold, and would linger on her nipples longer than was necessary to give them a firm pinch to attention when she thought it was needed.

"Okay, I expect to hear from you very soon, Hayley," Krystal barked into her phone. "We have the bitch, as promised – so now what?" She hung up the call with a vicious finger-stab at her phone's touchscreen as if whatever was irking her was entirely the cell's fault. She glowered across at Claire.

"Hayley?" Claire looked up at Krystal. "As in Hayley Barnett?" She allowed herself a smile. It all made sense now. Her gut instinct had been right; Hayley (and no doubt Farid and Garcia, too) *had* been up to something! She knew they could be a sly threesome but—this?

"Just goes to show, you can't trust anybody these days." Krystal gave Claire a sarcastic grin.

"That fucking bitch," Claire growled. "I should have known it." She uncrossed her legs again and saw Tony's eyes widen. "I wouldn't expect to be hearing from Ms. Barnett any time soon, though," Claire said to Krystal without emotion. "She's had a shit day."

"She'll be in touch," Krystal said and then turned to Tony. "And will you *please* concentrate on that fucking gun!" She barked.

"I am concentrating," Her husband protested with a whine. "It was *your* idea to keep her nude, Krystal."

"I kept her fucking naked to stop her running off." Krystal was getting angry. "Not so you can gawk at her fucking pubes!" She strode over to Tony and removed the gun from his possession, as one would a sharp object from a small child. "And who has fucking pubic hair anyway these days?" She sneered.

Claire looked down at the soft tuft that sprouted atop her mound and felt a little self-conscious. She'd never wholly understood the allure of the Full Brazilian look, and she didn't think that she would particularly want to be with a man who preferred his women to look like eight-year-old girls. Karl had always been happy with her natural, neatly trimmed bush.

Yeah, and just look how that turned out.

Claire turned her head as if someone had spoken those hateful words over her left shoulder. Of course, there was no one there. Krystal and her dipshit husband didn't appear to have heard anything either.

Dammit, now she was imagining things.

The doorbell rang, and this time Claire knew that she hadn't imagined that. All three in the house turned their heads in the direction of the front door, and there, a dark gray shape that looked decidedly human loomed large in the twin-stained glass windows.

"Who the fuck is that?" Tony glanced nervously towards the door and a slight nervous tic twitched in his left eye.

"How the hell should I know?" Krystal spat. "This is not my fucking house."

The doorbell rang again. And then a third time. Who ever was at the door was persistent, and evidently not going to go away anytime soon.

"You'd best go answer it." Krystal wiggled the gun at Claire.

There was a look in the woman's eyes that gave Claire a sick feeling in the pit of her stomach. "Sure," she gave her best shot at sounding nonchalant. "If I could just go get some clothes…"

"I think you are just fine as you are." Krystal gave a lascivious grin and looked Claire's exposed body up and down once again. "He's probably a God-botherer; you'll make his day."

Claire cringed. Whilst she was not ashamed of her body and had fewer hang-ups about it than most women she knew or had read about in Cosmopolitan, flashing strangers was something she drew the line at. She did figure, however, that this was all part of her captor's game, and they were both most likely getting off on the idea.

"I…I can't." She shook her head. "Please don't make me."

"Quit being such a pussy, Claire." Krystal grabbed Claire's arm and pulled her up off of the couch. "Go answer your door. Get rid of whoever that fucker is." Krystal pulled Claire towards the door. "And make sure that he sees the goodies." She poked Claire in the kidney with the cold gun barrel. "And don't forget that I'll be right behind you."

Claire padded over to the door, painfully aware that both Tony and Krystal were unashamedly ogling her bare ass as she walked. She could practically feel their perverted eyes burning into her flesh.

As she cracked open the door, Claire's initial reaction was to wonder just how come the photocopier salesman was at her house? She recognized the drab, gray suit, the sallow skin and the sad, haunted eyes that dazzled a piercing blue. He appeared to be wearing new shoes; black ones with the kind of shine that you only see when they're fresh from the box. The poor guy appeared to be uncomfortable in them, he shifted foot to foot, and the shoes' stiff leather squeaked a little each time.

The guy on her doorstep flashed Claire a reassuring, but fake smile and a very real badge.

"Detective Andy Raymond." He held the badge up to Claire's face. "Miss Claire Jepson?" He smiled again.

Claire poked her head through the door gap a little further, like a tortoise emerging from its shell after a fright. "Can I help you?" She nodded.

"I'd like to talk to you about Karl Hobbs," the cop said. "May I come in?"

Claire felt Krystal give her a hearty shove in the ribs with the gun, and she pulled open the door to show some shoulder and a bare foot.

"Is—is Karl okay?" Claire faked concern.

"I'm afraid not, Miss Jepson." Raymond put on his somber face. "I am sorry to have to inform you that we found what we believe to be Mr. Hobbs' remains this morning."

"Oh my God." Claire put a hand to her mouth to emulate shock and distress. She felt the gun stab at her back again, and she allowed the door to swing open a tad more and this time it revealed an entire bare leg and a tit. The tit in question, her right one, sported a stiff, angry nipple that pointed dark pink and accusing at the cop. Claire did manage somehow to contort herself behind the door to conceal her pussy, but she knew that it would now be fairly obvious to the man that she was naked.

"I was the one who found him," Raymond went on as if he hadn't actually realized he was talking to a naked woman. "Over at Randy's Motel on FM964. I'm sorry to be the one to break the news, Miss Jepson." The cop appeared nonplussed by Claire's unashamed display of nudity; perhaps naked women opened their doors to him on a daily basis? "I called in at your office earlier, but your security guy told me that you had gone home early." Raymond stepped closer to the door, and Claire saw him sniff at the air like a dog that's caught a rival's scent on a tree stump.

"I wasn't feeling too well," Claire told him.

"Your security guy, Mr. Foote," the cop said, "he was busy organizing some kind of clean up, so he wasn't too helpful." The cop gave Claire an odd look and snuck a glance down at her exposed breast.

The truth was, Ethan Foote had abandoned his station at the main reception to coordinate the cleaners' cleaning up of the mess left behind by the supposed burst sewer pipe in the boardroom, and Raymond had simply walked right on in. He'd had a good old sneak around the place and had seen—and smelled—the disgusting state of the boardroom.

Bearing in mind the nature of the demise of one Karl Hobbs, and the cloying, stinking pile in which they'd found his body, Raymond had found the unsavory occurrence at Jepson's office to be quite the coincidence.

And now here he was, confronted by the delightfully naturist, Clair Jepson, and the now all too familiar odor that wafted from inside of her home that reminded the Detective of upset stomachs and foreign foods and something else that he couldn't quite put his finger on. A disturbingly common theme was already running through this investigation.

"Mr. Hobbs' car was still in the motel lot, and we traced it back to here," the cop said.

"That can't be right," Claire replied. "His car is right there." She pointed at the white Panamera on the crushed gravel driveway in front of the house.

"The car at the motel was an '02 Impala," the cop recalled. "Perhaps Mr. Hobbs had another vehicle that you didn't know about?"

"It's always possible, but…"

"If you would like to put some clothes on, I'd like to come in and ask you a few questions," the cop interrupted.

Claire could feel Krystal caressing the knobbles of her spine with the gun, and she shivered. She pulled the door open the rest of the way and stood gloriously naked and totally exposed in front of the cop.

The warm outside air played over Claire's sensitive skin and made her nipples and pussy tingle. She saw the cop's eyes glance downward at her vagina, and she was grateful for the coverage that her neat pubic hair offered, no matter how scant.

"I—I'm a little busy at the moment, Detective." Claire's voice quivered slightly as she forced her eyes to meet his.

"Is everything alright, Miss?" Raymond sounded concerned and strained his neck to peer into the house.

"Yes," Claire said. "I'm just having a rough day, that's all," she made with a strained smile.

"I promise I won't take up too much of your time," the cop persisted and made a move forward. His new shoes squeaked their protest. "If I could just step in for a few-"

Krystal stepped out from behind the door, pushed Claire aside and aimed her gun at the cop's face.

"I asked you to do one fucking thing, bitch," she snarled at Claire. "One fucking thing!"

SEVEN

Krystal had tied the cop to one of the ornate carver chairs she'd had Tony drag in from the dining room. She'd used a couple of the white, plastic cable ties they'd brought along specifically for use in restraining Claire. She had fully intended to use them but then realized that the rich bitch was cooperative enough under the watchful gaze of the gun and had much more potential for fun and games untethered and naked. Krystal had relieved the cop of his gun, of course, and now both she and Tony had a weapon.

The balance of power was tipped firmly in their favor.

Detective Andy Raymond looked fed-up and pissed at himself. His wrists were strapped so tightly to the chair arms that the skin on his hands had already turned blue in just the twenty minutes since he'd been tied up.

Behind him, Krystal paced back and forth, cell phone pressed tightly to her ear. "Listen to me,

Barnett," she snarled the last word as if it were the most obscene word she knew in the English language. "You'd better get off of your fucking fat ass and call me straight back, otherwise there's a whole heap of fucking shit coming your way!" She thumbed the phone to hang up the call and threw it down on the couch. "What the fuck are you looking at?" she shouted at Claire's smirk.

Claire looked away and shuffled uncomfortably on the couch, her sweating buttocks clinging to the leather.

"It looks like you're having quite a run of bad luck for one person in one day, Miss Jepson," Detective Raymond said in an attempt at levity in absurd circumstances.

Claire gave a faint smile. "I guess you could call it that," she said.

"And there I was, thinking that you didn't appear as distressed as I thought you should be for someone who'd just been told her fiancé was dead." His eyes looked genuinely apologetic. "And all the time, you had these nice people over for a visit." He nodded towards Tony.

Tony returned the gesture with a grimace; the unfamiliar weight of the cop's gun was making his hand shake.

"Will you just shut the fuck up?" Krystal yelled at the cop. "I am trying to fucking think here!"

"Perhaps you should listen to what Miss Jepson is telling you." Raymond kept his voice calm, soft and level: *mediation 101*. "Hayley Barnett clearly isn't going to return your call, so you may want to consider an alternative exit strategy."

"Oh, I have already considered *several* of those," Krystal growled and paced towards Claire, gun waving.

"I meant one that involved all of us getting out of this alive."

"I can pay you, give you anything," Claire offered. "What do you want?"

Krystal stooped down and landed Claire a hard slap across the breasts. Claire squealed, and her tits jiggled wildly under the force of the assault. An instant red handprint appeared on the side of her left breast. "What I *want* is for you to keep your motherfucking mouth shut!" Krystal screamed in her face.

"Hey, babe," Tony called over to his wife, "calm down. We'll think of something." He patted the spot on the sofa next to himself and reached out his free hand for her to join him.

Krystal complied. Although not subservient, she knew that she did need to stay calm in order to be able to think straight.

"Do you know what happened to Miss Barnett?" Raymond—ever the fucking detective—asked Claire. "Did it have something to do with that shit storm in the boardroom?"

Claire shrugged. "All I know is that she and the other two board members were plotting to take over my company," she said. "My guess is that once she knew I was on to them, she skipped town. Or even the country," she added the last bit upon realizing she'd just given herself motive.

"All a bit sudden though, wasn't it?" The tenacious Raymond clearly wasn't buying her story. "And the mess…"

"The sewer pipe burst, that's all," Claire snapped. "And would you mind if we didn't talk about that now, please?" She could feel her stomach churning over in that all too familiar fashion, and she rubbed at her sore breast to take her mind from it. She was also not unaware that her nipples had puckered to stiff, wrinkled points, and she had gotten undeniably wet between the legs.

Krystal was staring at her, too, with a look that

made Claire feel scared, and Claire just couldn't shake the thought that the only way she'd be leaving her house again would be feet first and in a body bag.

"Okay." Krystal shot to her feet, her own eureka moment too good to deliver sitting down. "If Barnett is not going to come through for us, we'll just have to make our own payday."

"I already told you I'd pay you," Claire said.

"Yeah, but we're not interested in the crumbs, we want the whole fucking table." Krystal's voice was firm, terrifyingly calm. "I'm guessing that a rich cow like you will have a safe packed with goodies somewhere in the house."

Claire shook her head. "I don't…"

"And not just cash, either." Krystal ignored Claire's protests. "There'll be jewelry, property deeds, maybe even share certificates for that big ol' company of yours." She stood over Claire once more. Claire folded protective arms over her tits, not wishing to have them slapped a second time. "Am I getting warmer, Miss Jepson?"

"No," Claire protested. She shot a glance at Raymond, although what she expected him to do to help, she wasn't certain. "I don't have a safe. Everything's in a deposit box at the bank."

Krystal reached down between Claire's legs and grabbed herself a lock of silky black hair.

"I. Don't. Fucking. Believe. You." Krystal gave a progressively harder tug on Claire's pubic hair with each word.

"Ouch!" Claire yelped; the tug on the word *you* had wrenched a clump of hair from her mound and made her eyes—and pussy—water.

"I suggest that while we're waiting for Hayley-fucking-Barnett to call us back, we help Miss Jepson here to remember where her safe is." Krystal smiled at Tony.

"And we can have ourselves a little fun while we're at it." She dabbled a finger down into Claire's slit, and it came away slick and glistening. Krystal rubbed her wet finger against her thumb as if contemplating some precious substance. "What do you say, Miss Jepson?"

Claire looked up at the woman—and the gun in the woman's hand—and offered something of a reassuring expression. Yes, she'd do anything to stay breathing and to keep alive the hope of surviving this ordeal.

Anything.

And at that thought, Claire's stomach turned over with an audible *schloop*.

***

It was at around the same moment that Krystal was reminding herself that this entire caper was more about getting her perverse kicks than about the money that Claire's panicking mind hatched the beginnings of a plan.

"If Madame would care to join me," Krystal sneered. She knocked Claire's arms away from her chest and grabbed her right nipple with a firmness that brought forth an involuntary gasp. Krystal yanked on the nipple, and Claire rose to her feet and hissed in a sharp intake of breath through clenched teeth.

"I think it's high time we had some fun, don't you?" Krystal purred.

"I thought you'd never ask!" Tony leapt to his feet, an eager beaver look on his face.

"Not you, asshole!" Krystal snapped at him. "I said *we*." She pressed her lips onto Claire's and forced her tongue into her captive's mouth. At first, she felt resistance, and her probing tongue was met with the hardness of teeth, but once she began stroking Claire's moist labia with the gun, it was *open sesame.*

Krystal and Claire tongue-wrestled a while, while Tony and the cop had nothing to do but watch. Krystal tugged hard on Claire's sore nipple and took great delight in the soft groan that the action elicited. She kept the gun between Claire's thighs and massaged her clit with the hard steel. Occasionally, she would slip the gun's barrel inside Claire's sopping vagina. And when she did, Claire moaned into Krystal's mouth and parted her legs just a hint more.

All too aware that she had an audience, Claire did her best not to feel too self-conscious, and she thrust her tongue deep into Krystal's mouth with aplomb and groped around under the diminutive mini skirt until she found the hot, wet cunt that was swollen and inviting between Krystal's thighs. Claire played with the succulent flesh over the silky material of Krystal's panties as they kissed, her fingers wet and slippery with the juice that soaked through the kidnapper's gusset. She ventured a finger along the side seam, and slipped it with ease into Krystal's hole.

Claire felt Krystal's body relax with a moan, and the cold steel of the gun caress the inside of her own vagina, and she added a second finger to the first.

And then a third.

Krystal groaned and felt herself succumb to the pleasures of the woman's touch. Tony, Samuel—and indeed any of the myriad men she'd fucked over the years—would always pale into insignificance alongside the expertise of a female's fingers at her cunt; it had been far too long.

She was also delighted at just how compliant Claire had become with a gun pointing at her (*in her*), and Krystal wondered just how far she would be able to push the bitch before she gave up the safe she was so goddamned sure about.

"Lie down." Krystal commanded, as she broke her mouth away from Claire's with great reluctance. She guided Claire back on to the couch and this time had her recline.

Krystal lifted Claire's knees up and then pushed them wide apart to spread Claire's pussy open. Krystal then plunged her face into the wet, inviting flesh and drove her tongue deep into the gaping vagina.

Claire moaned out loud, no longer caring that Tony and the cop—*Raymond?* Was that his first name, or his second?—were gawking at her amateur lesbian show with dicks tenting their pants. She was so turned on right now, that she almost forgot all about her plan.

Krystal pulled back, her face a slippery wet mess that dripped with Claire's juices; she found it remarkable just how overactive the woman's Bartholin's gland had suddenly become. She twisted her head to address Tony.

"Stick your dick in the bitch's mouth." She instructed.

Needing no second asking, Tony Wyatt came straight over, unzipping his fly as he walked. By the time he'd made the end of the couch and knelt with one knee either side of Claire's head, his filthy penis was out and clutched firmly in hand.

"Put that stinking thing in her mouth." Krystal instructed with a dirty smile and looked up at the disgusted look on Claire's face.

Claire could smell the diseased cock when it was more than a yard away from her face, and the stink made her gag; she felt the acid sting of bile at the back of her throat and fought it down. Before she knew it, Tony's foul-tasting member was forcing itself between her lips where it left scabby scrapings on her teeth and jabbed at her uvula. She gagged once more.

"There's no need to do this." Detective Raymond tried to intervene. "You're just making things a whole lot worse." He gave a fruitless struggle against his restraints but knew he could do nothing but watch as Krystal pushed her head between Claire's thighs once again.

Krystal slurped eagerly at the crinkled vaginal flesh that greeted her. She pulled Claire's labia wide apart with one hand and strained her tongue 'till it ached to get as deep inside that flavorsome vagina as was humanly possible. Inside, she rolled it around the ridged flesh and lapped at the mucus like some thirsty wild animal. When she came up for air and looked up over Claire's enviable, flat stomach and generous mounds of breast, she could see Tony's dick sliding in and out of the woman's mouth.

Tony disengaged his cock from Claire's mouth. He was keen to not climax so early on in the game, since he had a gut feeling that there were more erotic delights yet to come. He shifted his position slightly and aimed his asshole over Claire's horrified face.

"Lick me out, rich bitch." Tony was really getting into character now. "Stick your tongue up my asshole."

Claire shook her head, as she contemplated the poorly wiped brown hole that hovered just inches from her eyes "No," she said.

"Do as you're told," Krystal growled, her face buried so deep into Claire's vulva that the words came out muffled and sounded more like wet farts.

"I can't," Claire protested. "Not that."

Krystal pulled her face clear. "Put your ass on her mouth, Tony."

Tony did as instructed, gripping Claire's head between his thighs to hold it in place. It still took several attempts before he hit the bull's-eye.

"Tell me if her tongue's not inside your anus."

Tony shook his head, feeling nothing but pursed lips

on the sensitive skin around his ass.

Krystal laid her gun on the couch and used her freed hand to spread Claire's pussy lips *really* wide apart. She stretched the engorged, elastic skin out and up to expose Claire's timid clitoris. Claire's clit popped so far out of its hood that it appeared circumcised, and she moaned against Tony's suffocating butt.

Krystal brought her other hand down hard on Claire's defenseless cunt, and the resounding *SLAP!* resonated around the room.

Raymond winced but couldn't tear his eyes away from the scene, disgusted at himself for feeling so fucking horny.

Claire cried out in agony/ecstasy and snaked her reluctant tongue upwards and into Tony's dirty asshole.

"Ooh." Tony's eyes rolled upwards, and he pushed down against the invading tongue.

Happy again, Krystal resumed dining at the Y. This time she substituted her aching tongue for a duo of probing fingers. Simultaneously, she worked hard at her own clit with her other hand.

Claire tried to keep her focus on the delightful waves of pleasure that emanated from her pussy, and not the foul taste that assaulted her taste buds and made her want nothing more than to vomit. It was not that she'd never given a rimjob before, in fact, Claire considered herself quite the connoisseur of the butt holes of *both* sexes—it was that Tony's was a revolting mess of unwiped fecal matter and tiny balled up bits of toilet tissue that were tangled up in the coarse hair around his anus. Even following funky flavors of his dick (*just where the fuck had he had that thing?!*), the dry, flaky crumbs of crap that dropped onto her face, which she inadvertently inhaled up her nose, were enough to make her guts turn somersaults. It was like snorting the cheapest, most shit-smelling ghetto cocaine known to man.

But still, despite all of that, and despite herself, Claire Jepson found herself on the brink of orgasm.

And then she came with a scream that blew air up into Tony's rectum and made him squeal, and with a wild bucking of her entire body threw Krystal—in the throes of her own orgasm—off of the sofa.

Claire sat up, breasts slick with sweat and heaving with labored breathing, her face flushed crimson. The tsunami of orgasm upon orgasm was still sweeping through her body, and her arms and legs felt weak and wobbly. And as the pleasure faded as quickly as it had arrived, Claire's mind cleared, and her eyes fell upon Krystal's carelessly abandoned gun.

"Don't even think about it." Tony tapped the cop's gun against the back of Claire's skull.

Claire turned her head to face him, her face dotted with his dried poop sprinkles, and his rancid prick almost jabbed her in the eye. "I wasn't thinking of *anything*," she lied.

Krystal regained her own senses, grabbed the gun and pointed it at Claire's face.

"Well done, my darling." Krystal smiled up at her husband with her face glistening shiny and wet.

"What I *was* thinking," Claire ventured as her breathing returned to its post-orgasm norm, "is that it looks like I am unlikely to get out of this…" she contemplated the word "*situation*." She let the idea hang between herself and her captors, her final surrender to their dominance. "So, there is something I always wanted to try out. I guess it's now or never." She gave a sheepish smile, and her mind flitted to the signals Krystal had given out throughout the course of the ordeal.

Claire hoped to God she'd read Mrs. Wyatt correctly.

"Happy to oblige," Krystal said, not even attempting to deny Claire's fatalism.

"Thank you." Claire played the submissive to perfection and lowered her eyes.

"Okay, spill." Tony was, as ever, over eager.

"Time's a'tickin', hun." Krystal smiled as if she and Claire, given different circumstances, could be the very greatest of friends and playmates.

"Have you guys ever seen *Two Girls, One Cup*?" Claire asked. And by the way in which Krystal's eyes lit up, Claire knew that the balance of power between them had all at once shifted in her favor.

EIGHT

And so it happened that Claire Jepson found herself squatting over Krystal Wyatt's eager face like she was taking a pee in the woods. Claire's head was facing her kidnapper's feet, and Tony, for his part, pointed both the gun and his dick at his captive's forehead.

Claire had tried to reassure Tony and his good lady wife that there really was no need for the weapon as she was having a great time and had no intention of trying to escape.

But sometimes there's just no trust between people.

Krystal had stripped off to stark naked in record time and lay back on the luxurious carpet. She gazed up at Claire's parted ass cheeks, at that exotic puckered brown knot that twitched and pulsed with all manner of delightful promise. Krystal fought the urge to lick and probe it with tongue and fingers, because, more than anything, she wanted to catch its sweet, sweet load in her mouth.

"You are a dirty, dirty toilet girl, aren't you?" Krystal purred at Claire with a playful lilt in her voice. "You gonna shit in Momma's mouth?"

"You bet your sweet fucking ass I am," Claire groaned, and Krystal could see Claire's anus relax and pout towards her open mouth as she began to push.

And as Krystal watched, she saw in delectable close up Claire's corn hole open up and the vivid red flash of the taut muscle tube as it peeped out like some timid woodland creature. It pursed outwards like an elderly maiden Aunt's lips and made ready to deliver its payload. Krystal moaned with delight as she saw the first hint of chocolate brown in the center of Claire's red flesh.

When it came, Claire's shit sputtered out of her in soft, thick strings that reminded Krystal of ice cream from a soft serve machine. It snaked out of Claire's bowels and coiled into Krystal's gaping mouth, and she gobbled it down with avarice. The taste and scent of the *caviar* conjured colorful memories of the most depraved of trysts in filthy public lavatories, oriental spices and—most peculiarly—the bukkake parties she and Tony used to frequent.

"Enough!" Krystal swallowed the last mouthful and pushed on Claire's butt to move her away, to get her to stop. As wonderful as it was, the seemingly endless stream had filled Krystal up and was threatening to choke her, so much so that she felt the uncontrollable panic of claustrophobia grip her, and she had to be free.

Claire slid down Krystal's chest and left a slimy trail of defecation between the woman's tits. She tensed her sphincter to pinch shut her anus and returned to her place on the sofa.

"That was freakin' awesome!" Tony enthused. He glanced over at the cop who sat quietly with a nauseated look of disbelief on his face. "What do you think, Detective?"

Raymond failed to give Tony the validation he was looking for, so Tony shot him in the foot. The cop screamed out and writhed in the chair, and blood poured out from his new shoe to soak into the shagpile.

"Tony!" Krystal admonished.

"I said, what do *you* think?" Tony repeated.

"Awesome," Raymond choked, his face contorted with pain.

"Never mind him." Krystal was still very much in the moment. "It's time for Scene Two." She plucked a small glass bowl from the side table that hugged the arm of the couch. She tipped out the potpourri and held the bowl under her chin. "You ready for this, dirty bitches?" She grinned a broad grin at Claire and Tony.

Claire nodded as eagerly as she could. The gunshot had scared her; the sudden explosion of violence in her home had been most unnerving. She'd now begun to doubt herself. What if the plan failed? If there hadn't been before, there was now no doubt in her mind that these people were perfectly capable of leaving no witnesses to their crimes.

Krystal contemplated the bowl, and the belly full of the sweetest tasting shit she'd ever eaten, and anticipated with great relish the next part of the game.

She poked a forefinger at the back of her throat and felt the sharpness of her fake nail scrape on her tonsils. One more prod and her gag reflex kicked in, she retched noisily, and her stomach began to empty itself.

The glass bowl filled quickly—much quicker than Krystal had anticipated—and soon overflowed. The lumpy liquid cascaded down her front and turned her tits a sickly, stinking brown. The stench of regurgitated excrement and stomach acid filled the room and made Krystal's guts turn over a second time.

By her fourth time, Krystal was dry-heaving, and the

entire contents of her stomach that had not made it to the bowl now lay down her front, on her thighs and in a spreading semi-circle on the floor. She heaved again and began choking.

Instinctively, she put her hands to her neck as her breathing was cut off, and her peripheral vision went black. She clawed at her throat and felt something hard in there that was making it bulge out as if she were doing some bizarre tropical frog impersonation.

"She's choking, for Christ's sakes!" She heard the cop through the intense ringing in her ears, which sounded like a dozen people blowing shrill whistles inside her head.

And then there were arms around her waist and firm, voluminous breasts pressed into her back. She felt the intense pressure as Claire gave her best shot at a Heimlich manoeuver.

Krystal retched and felt something *give* inside.

The lump in her throat coughed up and out of her mouth and was followed by more slippery stuff that left a tangy slime on her tongue.

"Fuck." She heard Tony say, and saw a look on his face that read utter horror.

Krystal glanced down and realized that she had thrown up her *actual* stomach. Behind it, streaming from her gaping mouth like a steam locomotive from a tunnel came the rest of her digestive system.

The gray-blue bag of Krystal's stomach slopped onto her legs and slid wetly to the carpet like a beached jellyfish. Attached to it were the pink snakes of her intestines, which jostled from her in an endless stream of glistening slime to coil around her knees. Krystal could do nothing; she sat rooted to the spot and made a feeble attempt to catch her guts as they gushed from her. But they simply slipped through her trembling hands.

By the time Krystal's colon—ascending, descending *and* transverse—had slithered from her mouth, all her fading mind could think was *this is me, puking my fucking guts up*.

Krystal Wyatt coughed out her rectum followed by its attached anus. Her brain took this as its cue to mercifully switch itself to 'off', and her wasted body slumped to the floor in the slippery pile of viscera.

Claire, Tony and Detective Raymond sat open-mouthed and helpless as the entire thing played out. It was as if Krystal had transformed into a particularly gruesome burlesque performer, and now that her act was over, she'd pick herself up and take that well-earned bow.

"What the fuck happened to her?" Tony stood up and pointed his gun at Claire. "What did you do to my fucking wife?!"

Claire put up her hands in a defensive gesture and shook her head.

"I didn't…"

The foul mess began to move. The thick, brown liquid and spilled innards that Krystal had puked was pooling together and beginning to rise up in a thick, clumpy column between Claire and Tony. As the shit rose up, it sucked itself out of the carpet like a kid sucking up milkshake through a straw, and it absorbed Krystal's body into its mass from a thick rope of itself that intruded into her wrecked asshole.

And so, the pile of shit grew taller, stronger, and began to take shape. As it did so, Krystal's corpse sagged and deflated, as the entity digested her from the inside.

By this point, words had completely abandoned Tony Wyatt, and all his mouth could do was flap open and shut soundlessly. Instead, he let the gun do his talking. It buckled wildly in his hand, as he emptied round after round into the expanding mass of stink that loomed over him. The bullets hit the thing square on with a *splat splat splat* and were simply absorbed; they never even slowed the thing down.

When Tony got to that soul-crushing, final click of the empty clip, he threw the gun at the thing in one final act of defiance.

A thick tendril roped out from the shit-monster and grabbed Tony firmly by the wrist. He squealed like a kindergartner with his foreskin trapped in his zipper and struggled in vain against the thing that had a firm hold of him.

Claire took as many steps back as she could behind Raymond's chair, until she felt the hard wall against her back. As repulsed as she was at the thing she had deliberately summoned, she couldn't help but stare.

For now, it had formed into an approximation of a man's shape, constantly shifting and oozing against the pull of gravity. As Claire watched, she saw Krystal's body reduce to little more than a skin suit, and the shit pile seemed to become a little more solid.

More *human*.

It then pulled the yowling Tony Wyatt into its now semi-solid body like he was a lassoed rodeo calf. The thing ignored his pitiful pleading that none of this was his idea, and could it let him go – *pleeeese?* It pressed Tony's wriggling body into its own stinking shape, and more tendrils shot out to embrace the struggling man.

Tony's final screams were muffled to almost nothing, as the shit flowed into his mouth, his nose, and on down his throat. Unlike his wife, Tony was digested and absorbed from the outside in, as his flesh effervesced and dissolved under the shit's embrace. As his limp body was rapidly assimilated into the animated pile of excrement, the thing's shape looked even more defined than before, and its covering began to look less like drying crap and more like smooth, pink skin.

Claire turned away as the back of Tony's head dissolved, and his brains slopped out onto her floor. She couldn't help herself but flick through her mental Rolodex to find 'C - Carpet Cleaners'.

When Tony Wyatt was completely gone, the thing turned around to face Claire. It stepped over what little remained of Tony's spouse on legs that looked strong and muscular.

"Hello again, Claire," it said in that familiar, cheeky-chappie accent, and it flashed its set of perfect pearly-whites and startling eyes. And Claire noted that its eyes had mismatched irises—one brown, one blue—and she recalled only ever having seen that once before...

"Oh my God," she stammered.

"It's good to see you, as always." The thing smiled.

Claire tried to speak again, but couldn't. All she could do was gawk at the thing like some love-struck teenager meeting her favorite boy band, and she noticed that the naked man-shaped thing that had formed itself from the crap she'd fed to Krystal Wyatt was entirely hairless, hung like a fucking horse and had real finger and toenails.

"Who...what is that?" Detective Raymond spoke up. His voice was strained, his face white. He'd lost—and was still losing—a lot of blood from the wound in his foot.

"I wouldn't know where to begin," the thing said, as it extended an arm towards the cop and grasped his hand.

"No!" Claire screamed. "Don't!"

"Calm down, sweetheart!" It laughed at her. And then to Raymond, "I am Richard Richard the Third. How do you do, Detective Raymond?" It shook the cop's tethered hand the best it could against the restriction of the cable ties.

Claire could see the look of disgust on the cop's face at

the touch of the thing's (she couldn't think of it as a *'Richard'*) flesh.

The cop could do nothing more than gaze up at Richard Richard III with a dumbfuck look on his face. "Could you please untie me now?" He asked.

***

"All in good time, mate." Richard's voice adopted that singsong cockney lilt that so jangled Claire's nerves. "That very much depends on my best girl." It sidestepped the cop and approached Claire.

Claire once again felt very naked, very vulnerable, and incredibly turned on. She was finding it a struggle to tear her eyes away from the monstrous, dangling prick that swayed hypnotically back and forth, back and forth as the thing—*Richard*—walked towards her. And when she did lift her eyes upward, they traced their way up along his toned, muscular torso, across his broad shoulders and to his beautiful face.

Jesus H, he—*it*—was gorgeous. If ever Leonardo DiCaprio and Johnny Depp were to have anal sex and shit out a love child, it would look like this *man* that Claire had created with her waste. She gazed at the look of wanton lust in Richard's eyes and felt a viscous trickle of pussy juice make its way down along the inside of her thigh.

Then Richard was standing before her, achingly near and in all his glory. To Claire, he was her perfect fantasy of manhood, and he was so close that she could feel his warm breath on her skin and smell his slight-but-pungent odor of rot and decay. She'd found his odor off-putting at first, but soon found herself growing used to it, enjoying it even. She knew that the human nose would learn to ignore a persistent smell in time, to the point where the scent would fade to nothing. As her Granny used to say, *it was either that or the whole world would smell of snot.*

"Please," Richard implored, his eyes searching Claire's. "Don't let all of—*this*—override the way I know you feel right now." He smiled. "Give me a chance?"

Claire gazed up at him and wanted more than anything to cram his huge, dangling dick into her vagina.

"Come on." Richard dazzled her with a flash of his oh-so-perfect teeth. "What have you got to lose? Didn't you say that all men were shit anyways?" He spread his arms to his sides, palms up in the universal *trust me* gesture.

Claire flinched at the comment. He was right, of course, but she had actually *thought* it. Could he read her mind, too?

"Of course, I can," Richard replied. "I know everything that goes on in your head because I am all yours, Claire." Richard's voice was velvet smooth like the finest chocolate. "Quite literally, as a matter of fact." He beamed as if deliriously pleased with himself. "I can give you experiences and sensations beyond your wildest dreams, every sexual desire and perversion that you could possibly imagine." He reached out and traced one perfectly formed finger down along her breast. "And many others that you couldn't even begin to imagine." He gave her a cryptic look and cupped her tit in his slender hand. "Yet."

At first, Claire cringed at Richard's touch and regretted her decision to retreat to the wall, as she had no place else to go. But as he caressed her with the featherweight touch of his cool, waxy skin and held her breast in his palm something deep and dark inside of her tingled.

Despite the fact that she knew what he—it—was made of.

"I've heard all that before." Claire gave a cynical look. Richard's speech was not so much different than the one Karl had seduced her with.

And look at how that turned out.

"I know."

"You're just like every other man I've met." Claire felt her anger rising, which she found to be in inverse proportion to the wonderful throb in her vagina. "You're just so full of…"

She paused.

"Go on, say it." Richard smiled at her embarrassment. "You know you want to."

"Shit," she said quietly. "You're so full of shit." She slapped his chest with the flat of her hand, and his body felt firm and masculine.

And then they laughed together: ice broken.

Richard bowed his head and pressed his lips to Claire's left breast. He rolled her stiff nipple around in his mouth like it was a piece of sweet, hard candy. Claire groaned and felt her knees go weak and threaten to spill her onto the floor. She gripped Richard's shoulders for support, and over the shiny dome of his naked head, she saw the cop looking at her with a look of absolute disgust that shone through his pain.

Richard pulled away from the nipple. As he did so, he nibbled at it between his teeth to stretch it out, and Claire had to mentally restrain herself from pushing his head back to her bosom for more.

He kissed her.

His lips were soft and pliable and moulded themselves around hers, and his invading tongue tasted metallic in her mouth. It was a taste of flesh that reminded her of uncooked steak.

Without warning, Richard's dick had found its way to her pussy. It snaked towards its goal as if it had a mind of its own and probed at the soft wet flesh to nudge at her throbbing clitoris, until she tilted her hips to meet his gentle thrust. Then, with a subtle increase in pressure, he slipped inside her, and Claire let out a groan so deep, so intense, that she startled herself.

"Is that okay?" Richard murmured against her lips.

"Very," Claire replied, although she ached for the feeling of being filled to capacity down there.

"No problem." Apparently, Richard really could read her thoughts. Made sense, she figured, as she relaxed into the moment.

Richard picked her up, and she wrapped her firm thighs around him. He lowered her gently to the couch, and the leather made for a cool contrast to the sweat-dampened skin on her back. He pushed his hips against hers and held still.

Claire could feel his cock growing inside her. It felt so weirdly different to the guys who were usually so eager to sink into her that they didn't get really hard until they were actually fucking. In contrast, the sensation was as if Richard's dick was expanding in both length and girth to *fit* her vagina perfectly. She closed her eyes to concentrate upon the heavenly feel of being filled up from the inside that rolled through her body. She could feel every inch, every ounce, every wrinkle of flesh of that magnificent cock, as it bulged into the precise size and shape required to hit her g-spot, her a-spot—*all* of her fucking spots!

Richard slid his thickened penis in and out of her with steady, deliberate movements that were orchestrated to grind his pubic bone against her stiffened clit, and Claire's body shuddered with ecstasy overload.

As Richard pumped away at her squelching cunt, Claire slid her hands over his toned body, eager to experience every delicious inch of her new lover. His skin felt so good—strange, but delicious—almost like genuine skin, albeit a little clammy to the touch and apt to crumble away in places. Nonetheless, she found herself enjoying the malleable, waxy feel of Richard's flesh and the way it made her feel so delightfully dirty.

"I'm almost done," Richard whispered in her ear.

"That's okay." Claire couldn't hide the disappointment in her voice.

"I don't mean this." He slipped his dick out of her and slid its slippery head over her slit. "I mean me. I just need to take in one more person, two at the most. Then I'll be *completely* human." He glanced over his shoulder at the cop, who was watching the free sex show through drooping eyelids.

"No." Claire was horrified that Richard would lay that choice at her feet, especially at a moment such as this.

Richard plunged his cock back inside Claire's vagina and smiled as she gasped out loud and dug her nails into his shoulders.

"But, just think of what I have to offer you, Claire," Richard persisted, his voice so full of lascivious promise.

"Tell me." Claire was breathy, panting.

"Well, there's this."

Claire felt the cock that had her cunt stretched to capacity suddenly shrinking, and she moaned her protest. Richard's dick diminished with such lightning speed that it slipped out of her with a vibrant *slurp*.

"Bastard," She grumbled and slapped at Richard's chest. There, her hands slapped against the firmest, most bountiful pair of breasts she had ever felt; magnificent orbs with smooth skin so pale and translucent that she could see the intricate patterns the thin blue veins made beneath it. Aroused beyond all reason, Claire couldn't help but caress the tits that hung down to touch her body, and she rubbed the bullet-hard nipples against her own.

And then the tits were snatched away from her playful fingers as Richard maneuvered his groin and that once superlative dick up towards her face.

Only there was no dick.

Claire found herself faced with the most appetizing cunt she thought she had ever been acquainted with. It was totally denuded—of course—and had fleshy outer lips that were puffed out in arousal like an exotic orchid. Richard's inner lips protruded sweetly and were spread out like a delicate butterfly to expose the glistening clit and dark entrance to an incredibly tight vagina.

Animal desire overtook Claire, and she couldn't help herself. She pulled on Richard's hips to guide him/her onto her mouth and buried her head in the freshly formed pussy, to gorge herself on the moist flesh and its faint piscine perfume.

"I can be even more human than *this*. I can be anyone, anything you want me to be," Richard purred and reached behind himself to apply expert fingers to Claire's drenched pussy. She bucked and writhed beneath him, and he heard her say a dampened *okay* through her mouthful of flesh.

Claire couldn't see the slender brown tendril that snaked out of Richard's ass and zigzagged its way towards the helpless detective. It slithered across the smooth, flat of her stomach—she *felt* that—and darted at Detective Andy Raymond like an angry cobra. Claire didn't hear the man's screams as the thing burrowed into his eye socket and drilled itself up into his brain to suck it clean from his skull, because Richard had his thighs pressed tight against her ears.

Richard turned his head to watch the detective's demise. He had a ravenous look upon his face, as if he were facing his first meal in a long, long time. Raymond was already weak with blood loss from his foot, but he mustered the last of his energies to struggle against his assailant. However, he could do little more than kick and jerk the chair until it toppled over onto its side with a hollow *thunk*.

As Richard watched the detective's demise, he never once broke tempo on Claire's engorged clitoris. He saw the detective's body spasm like a pitched frog, as his head was digested from the inside and within a minute or so, Detective Raymond's skull crumpled in on itself like a doorstep pumpkin a week after Halloween, and putrid fecal matter bubbled from his nose.

Oblivious to the fate she had sealed for the detective, Claire slurped at the prolific pussy on her face. She drank down the scrumptious, oozing juice that dribbled from the hot, soft flesh like honey from its comb. She used probing fingers to pull the pussy lips wide apart to better feel the raw flesh on her face and to force her tongue ever deeper inside the rawness of her lover's newly formed vagina.

As she lost herself in the feel, the smell, the smothering closeness, Claire could feel Richard's pussy begin a subtle metamorphosis. That faint, but oh so delectable aroma of defecation faded away to nothing, the skin felt firmer, the wet flesh beyond the swollen lips more…

…*solid*.

Denial be damned, Claire knew precisely the reason for her lover's transformation, and that the detective wouldn't be there when she resurfaced.

And she really didn't give a shit.

Claire felt another change in the genitalia that sucked at her face, and this time it was far less subtle. Richard's exquisite vagina bulged outwards to revert back to that hard, insistent cock. It throbbed and twitched, as it pushed its way into Claire's mouth and way down to the back of her throat to challenge her gag reflex. She felt the smooth weight of Richard's balls banging against her slick chin, and she tipped her head back to give the dick free passage along her gullet.

Then she gagged, and her lover pulled out with an apology, and replaced his dick with his mouth and tender kisses.

Richard lowered himself once more between Claire's gaping thighs. He placed a hand beneath each of her buttocks and tipped them ever so slightly upwards.

She felt the heat of his penis as it jabbed gently first at her pussy and then at her ass.

And then he was back inside her, and she had that mind-blowing *stuffed* sensation again, as Richard's cock expanded to mold itself to her every fold and crevasse, every contour of her anus and rectum. Claire was exquisitely aware of it creeping up into her, and she gasped with sheer pleasure when it pushed its way gently through the yielding sphincter at the far reaches of her rectum. Onwards, upwards into Claire's body, Richard's, swelling cock filled her fit to burst.

The stretched, full sensations that emanated from her gut washed wave upon wave of intense delight over Claire. Her mind raced with a thousand depraved thoughts, and she decided there and then that although she loved having her cunt fucked, she much preferred this variety of sex. It was perversely invasive and infinitely more penetrating.

More *intimate*.

All of Claire's letdown at the loss of Richard's scrumptious pussy in her mouth flew from her head, as he pushed and pulled, pushed and pulled and his sensuous cock slid in and out of her ass and expanded its way up inside her body.

Claire let out a cry, and forgetting that her new lover was completely bald, Claire reached up to pull on his hair; she had a penchant for hair pulling.

"One *more* person and I will have hair that you can

pull 'till it comes out by the roots." Richard nuzzled her ear lobe and nibbled it with teasing teeth.

Claire stroked the sweat-slicked scalp and inhaled the erotic, earthy stink of the lover she had conjured from her own excrement. "My cleaner will be here at six," she said with a deep, dirty growl. "You can screw my ass 'till then."

James H Longmore

...and Then You Die

ONE YEAR LATER

James H Longmore

NINE

"Ya must mean that snooty Mrs. Double-barrel, who thinks she's too freakin' good to live in a trailer park with the likes o' us?" The fat, greasy-skinned man said to the detective, his fried chicken breath assaulting her nostrils.

"Claire Jepson-Richards?" Detective Skyler Howgard lifted up the photograph she held tightly in her left hand, so it was a tad closer to the fat guy's piggy eyes. As if the stink from his rotted-tooth mouth wasn't bad enough, her nose was already stinging from the acrid stink of body odor that wafted over in thick waves from his corpulent frame.

"That's what I said." Fat guy seemed impatient; like he had a more pressing engagement inside his gloomy trailer with a football game, a six-pack of something cheap, and a family-sized pizza. "She's in the third trailer along on the left." He waved his flabby hand about in a non-specific direction for just in case his description hadn't been thorough enough. This served to generate a fresh wave of reek from the stained folds of his armpit. "Lives there with that piece of shit husband of hers." He grimaced.

Detective Howgard thanked the man and walked away from the trailer. As she did so, she drew in welcome gulps of fresh air in an attempt to rid her nose of the clinging smell. Little did she know, but the obese caretaker of the Raining Oaks Trailer Park wouldn't be the worse thing she'd smell that day.

Behind her, the fat guy's door closed in the detective's face with a resounding slam, and she could hear his TV booming even louder, as if he'd cranked up the volume to block her out. Howgard shrugged it off and made her way along the crushed rock driveway towards the third trailer on the left, her tan cowboy boots kicking up plumes of dust and oily grit as she walked.

The trailer park was a far cry from the salubrious setting in which Howgard had last interviewed Claire Jepson (*Jepson-Richards* as it was now, the detective reminded herself—the entrepreneur had gotten herself hitched not long before her business empire had gone so far down the toilet it was practically in the damned ocean). In cruel contrast to the magnificent house that was set in impeccably manicured gardens, Raining Oaks was populated with an untidy array of grubby, past-their-best trailers that were set amongst scrubby tufts of unkempt grass, seeding ragweed, and dog turds.

Arriving at the door to the Jepson-Richards trailer, Howgard rapped her knuckles hard on the plywood door that sported what looked very much like boot scuffs on its lower portion. She straightened her back – she had always had been prone to stooping, having been the tallest girl in her class since sixth grade—and stood to her full five-nine on the trailer's steps.

The door opened a tad, with a squeaky whine, and a pale, gaunt face peered out from the badly lit interior.

"Yes?" Claire enquired, as she screwed her eyes up against the harsh midday light that invaded her blanketing gloom.

"I don't know if you remember me, Miss. Jepson." The detective lifted up her badge for Claire to see. "We spoke last year about…"

"Detective Howgard?" Was that a smile? "Of course, I remember you. Please, come on in." Claire pulled open the trailer's rickety door to welcome the detective.

The first thing the detective noticed as the door swung open with a loud, complaining squeak was the faint, rich smell of decay and backed-up sewers that coated the inside of the double-wide; the second was that Claire Jepson (*Richards*!) was incredibly and most undeniably pregnant.

"You'll have to forgive the clutter," Claire apologized, although the living room seemed to Howgard to be remarkably uncluttered. "It's not so easy for me to keep on top of things these days." She stroked her immense belly over her gray sweats that looked like she'd been living in them since she'd conceived. "I tend to tire out quicker than I'd like."

"There's no need to apologize," the detective reassured. "How far along are you?"

"Eight months and counting." Claire gave her a weak smile, as if genuinely sorry for the fact that in a month's time she'd be squeezing another human being out through her vagina.

Howgard made herself comfortable on the threadbare velour couch that was the sickly color of diarrhea and had springs sticking up into the cushions. From her vantage point, she contemplated Claire as she fussed around in the kitchenette to fix them both a glass of iced water. *How the mighty have fallen*, the detective thought to herself; the first time she'd met with the Jepson woman had been shortly after the rather odd death of her fiancé and the disappearance of Detective Andy Raymond. Then, Jepson had looked intimidatingly sharp in her crisp, navy-blue Chanel suit and thousand-dollar shoes – the ones with the red soles. Now, the poor gal looked more like a beached whale in her stained sweatpants and top. Her bare feet looked dirty and rough, and there was chipped polish on her toenails. Add to that the greasy straggles of unwashed hair that flopped about Claire's face, and Howgard was almost feeling sorry for her.

"Here we go." Claire plopped two glasses of iced water onto the low, glass-topped table in front of Howgard. She eased her bulky frame down beside the detective with a grunt and what could easily have been a wheezy fart. "Now, how can I help you?"

"I was hoping that you may be able to help me with the case," Howgard began. "I'm revisiting the file since some new evidence has come to light," She lied; the case was as cold as it had been a year ago, and she'd just wanted to rattle the Jepson woman's tree a little and see what fell out.

"Really?" If Claire was surprised—or concerned—to hear Howgard's news, her face didn't show it. "Have you found Karl's killer?"

Howgard shook her head. "I'm afraid not..."

"Has Hayley Barnett turned up?"

"No." Again with the shake of the head.

"Farid or Edson?" Claire looked puzzled. "Surely you have a lead on one of them by now?"

"I really can't tell you anything new at this stage in the investigation, Miss Jepson-"

"Jepson-Richards, I got married." Claire flashed her cheap wedding band at the detective, in much the same way as she had brandished her badge.

"I'm sorry." Howgard smiled. "Congratulations, by the

way." She looked around the trailer, as if half-expecting the husband to magically appear from the shadows as if on cue.

"He's out," Claire said as if she'd read the detective's mind. "Looking for work." The truth was that Claire had no idea where Richard was, nor what he was up to – although she could have made a pretty good guess. And, in all honesty, she didn't much care these days; she was glad to have his sorry ass out of the trailer.

Things had not gone well for Claire following the events of that particular day, a little over twelve months ago, when her soiled underpants had first struck up a conversation with her.

Firstly, she had taken her eye off the ball with Jepson Software Solutions LLC, following the accusations that had flown thick and fast following the mysterious disappearance of all three of her board executives. Stock market confidence had plummeted, and her shares were off-loaded wholesale and dropped like the proverbial hot potato.

Shortly thereafter, Claire had discovered that Hayley Barnett had been siphoning off considerable amounts of company cash into numerous offshore accounts that nobody seemed to be able to trace. Whilst that did have the advantage of helping provide a tenuous explanation as to where the confounded woman and her cohorts might have got to (it was hypothesized a remote country with no extradition treaty – quite possibly Cuba) and halted the police investigation after three months, it had sounded the death knell for the business Claire had built up so diligently. Oh yeah, and it attracted the attention of the IRS. The upshot of the latter was a bill for one hundred fifty million dollars that Claire had no hope in hell of ever paying—and the inevitable bankruptcy that followed.

Secondly, there had been Richard. At first, the mind-blowing sex had been everything; it had certainly taken Claire's mind off of the complete and utter collapse of everything she had worked for. And despite his somewhat unorthodox origins, Richard had been at first a caring and attentive husband, her rock when everyone around her abandoned the sinking Jepson ship and Claire's world had crumbled. The sex had been astounding, Richard had given her everything she'd wanted—man, woman or true hermaphrodite—he'd spoiled her rotten, and for that, she could turn a blind eye away from just about anything

Sadly, things had turned to crap once she'd found herself to be pregnant; it really was amazing just how quickly the shiny veneer can come off of a romance, even one with an otherworldly being.

The child wasn't Richard's—that would have been impossible, what with him not being human and all, and his kind simply didn't reproduce that way—it was the result of a casual anal sex hook up that had gone astray. The guy they had taken home with them—back when Claire had still lived in the big house in which the detective and her unfortunate kidnappers had met their end—had accidentally slipped whilst sodomizing Claire at Richard's behest, and his dick had gone into her 'wrong' hole. The poor guy had looked mortified and hadn't been able to apologize enough!

Richard's interest in Claire had dropped off as quickly as if someone had flicked the *off* switch. Sure, he still fucked her from time to time, and it was as inventive and orgasmic as it used to be, but Claire could feel all too well that the spark had most definitely blown out. That, coupled with Richard's sudden need to go out by himself—his excuse being he needed to feed himself and bring home the money they needed to live (two birds, one stone and all that)—it didn't take much for Claire to deduce that her new husband was dallying outside of the marriage. In fact, it seemed to Claire that nowadays she was only good enough for Richard when he had been so drunk as to be unsuccessful in his philandering or when he needed her as bait in the seedy underground clubs he enjoyed frequenting. Many of the men at those particular clubs would go wild for hugely pregnant women with lactating breasts, and that made them easy prey for Richard.

Richard did, however, display an oddly paternal interest in the health of Claire's child, which she found quite endearing. Upon receiving her news, Richard had made Claire quit smoking and alcohol, and insisted she eat well; it was an attitude inversely proportional to how he treated *her*.

If she could have left Richard, Claire would undoubtedly have done so by now. However, in her current state she was entirely dependent upon him, both emotionally and financially—who the fuck was going to employ an eight-month pregnant bankrupt with an IRS investigation hanging over her head like the sword of Damocles?

"So, this new evidence?" Claire smiled her best disarming smile at the detective, keen to find out what the woman actually did know, if anything.

"We think we may have a lead on Detective Raymond's disappearance," Howgard lied to Claire once again. "Could you tell me what your relationship was with Ethan Foote?"

Claire snorted and iced water almost came out of her nose. She plonked her glass down hard on the table, and the ice cubes chinked together as if they were dancing. It had been quite a while since she'd heard that name, let alone thought about the man. "He was my security manager," she told the detective.

"I understand that he may have been more than that, Mrs. Jepson-Richards." Howgard was sounding confrontational now, as if she *did* know something.

"He was an old high school boyfriend; I felt sorry for him and gave him a job."

"That's not all you gave him, though, is it?" The detective made eye contact with Claire and held it.

"Okay, so we fucked on occasion; he gave me sexual relief when I needed it," Claire said without embarrassment. "I told your colleagues that much last year."

"Foote was possibly the last person to see Detective Raymond alive; they spoke at your offices on the day of his disappearance."

"And why would you think that Ethan had anything to do with that?" Claire was getting exasperated. She'd been around these particular houses last year with several of Howgard's colleagues and really failed to see the benefit of doing so again; it was becoming clear that the detective didn't actually have any fresh evidence at all.

"To protect you?" Howgard was fishing, of course.

"From what, detective?" Claire folded her arms across her formidable belly, as if to signify that this particular conversation was coming to a rapid end.

"That's what I intend to find out, Mrs. Jepson-Richards," Howgard all but snarled that last word.

Claire maintained her poker face, content that the detective knew nothing and was simply trying to get a rise out of her. On the day in question, Richard had disposed of Detective Raymond's car as proficiently as he'd absorbed the detective's body, although to this day Claire hadn't asked him precisely what he'd done with the thing.

At that point, the trailer door bashed open, and Richard stumbled in. He was clearly drunk and high as the proverbial kite on something that made him stink of chemicals.

Startled by the sudden intrusion, Howgard twisted her head around to greet the elusive Richard Richards.

"Who the fuck is this?" Richard growled as he slammed the door shut behind him.

"Detective Howgard." Claire looked more than a little afraid of her husband, although Howgard had noted that Claire hadn't even flinched when Richard crashed through the door; it was quite possible she was used to this type of behavior?

"Pleased to meet you, Mr. Richards." Howgard stood up and offered a hand. She thought that, aside from being inebriated, Richards actually looked quite sick, his pupils dilated so wide as to make his eyes look completely black. Also, Richards' tanned skin had a moist, waxy look to it, and he had a sickly, earthy smell about him, which reminded Howgard of stale underwear.

"Fucking cops." Richard ignored Howgard's hand and leaned against the thin cooker. "I thought we'd seen the last of you lot."

"Richard, she is a detective, not a cop and has been asking questions about the detective who disappeared last year," Claire explained. "I told her I don't remember anything more."

"Then it's time she was going, don't you think?" Richard glowered at Howgard.

"I'd like to ask you a few questions, Mr. Richards-"

"Do you have a warrant to be here?" Richard raised his voice.

"No, but your wife was kind enough to invite me in." Howgard offered a placatory smile.

"What are you, a fucking vampire?" Richard giggled at his own joke and seemed rather pleased with himself. "You need to leave now, lady."

Howgard looked down at Claire, who sat impassively on the couch, staring off into mid space, as if she had willfully disconnected from the mounting confrontation.

"Come back when you get a fucking warrant," Richard grumbled at the detective. "Me and the wife are going out to a club tonight, and I'm sure you can imagine the fucking age it takes for her to make herself presentable these days." He pointed at Claire's belly as if for emphasis. "That reminds me," he addressed Claire. "Wear this." He pulled a small, black dress from his pocket - a garment so flimsy that it *fit* in his pocket—and threw it at his wife. "It's that stretchy stuff, so it should go over your gut."

Claire lifted up the dress for inspection. It was minimal, incredibly short, with no back. It appeared to plunge down to somewhere below the waist and had just two thin strips of material that would obviously struggle to cover her swollen breasts. The dress also looked as if it had been worn before.

Richard pulled open the door. "So, if you would kindly *fuck off*, Detective." He pointed to outside, just to make sure she understood what was required of her.

Howgard fixed Claire with a stern face. She placed her small, white calling card on the table and made her way towards the door. "Don't leave town, Mrs. Jepson-"

"She won't," Richards barked, and all but manhandled Howgard out of the trailer.

As the door slammed shut behind her, Howgard clumped down the wooden steps. She had a gut feeling that there was more going on in that trailer than Jepson-Richards was letting on, apart from the obvious abuse from that jerk of a husband, of course. Howgard made a mental note to pay another visit to the wonderful Jepson-Richards very soon. She was confident that if she could get Claire on her own for long enough, she'd get her to crack.

As Howgard made her way across the dusty verge back

towards where she'd parked up, she knelt down by Richard's car—a beige rust-bucket of a Camry—and secreted a magnetic GPS tracker under the rear wheel arch. It was totally against protocol without the appropriate paperwork, but Howgard had a gut feeling that now she'd made herself known to Claire and the obnoxious Mr. Richards, it would behoove her to find out their precise movements over the next few days or so—she had a feeling that they may just be on the move before long.

Job done, Detective Howgard dusted off her jeans at the knees and hurried away.

TEN

The scat play club was a new one to Claire and Richard; it had just started up in an abandoned abattoir out of town, and it attracted a crowd to whom they were unknown. The clubs they had regularly attended over the past twelve months—those that were still going; they did have a tendency to disappear as quickly as they popped up—had become somewhat stale for Richard and Claire, and the pickings therein had been growing somewhat thin. It was almost as if the club patrons were finally picking up on the correlation between those who played with the increasingly pregnant woman and her tall, handsome husband and those who never returned to the club. This was a frustration to Richard, as it meant that they had to go farther afield to seek out suitable prey as it was so much easier to pick out victims from the club environment than to pick up streetwalkers—the police were all over that profession as it was.

It had transpired that Richard needed to feed every few weeks or so, something that Claire had only found out after living with him in the trailer for a couple of months. Having absorbed the detective and the two dumbest kidnappers in history, Richard's human form had remained stable for quite some time afterwards. Once that particular nourishment had worn off, Richard had begun reverting to his true shape (or lack thereof) and had a tendency to leave disgusting stains around the trailer, which he also had the unfortunate tendency to stink up between his meals.

So, in order to maintain Richard's human appearance, it had become a necessary part of the Jepson-Richards' routine to cruise the filthy underground clubs for prey; scat clubs were especially suited to this purpose, because the clientele tended to be transient, and no one noticed or cared all that much if they never returned. There was also the added benefit that the various stinks associated with watersports, scat, and emetophillia tended to hide Richard's fecal odor, and thus he was free to hunt for all the fresh meat he needed.

Claire had noted that of late, Richard had been venturing out more and more by himself, and more frequently than his necessity to remain human warranted; her conclusion was that he was fucking (as opposed to killing) for the enjoyment of it, because the thrill of the chase appealed to his over-inflated ego. And the saddest thing of all was that Claire was able to switch her mind off of the fact that her husband was going with other women - and men – as well as being a complete shit to her. The truth was that the more human Richard became, the more *in*human he seemed to be, and the less she could stand being anywhere near him.

It had come to a point now that Richard would only take Claire out with him when he was desperate to feed and required her not only to get into the clubs, but also to approach his unwitting victims. Experience had taught him that their fellow club goers were far more likely to get friendly with a lady - a pregnant one especially—than a guy on his own. And it was amazing just how many men (and women) went batshit crazy for a fat belly and freely lactating tits.

Richard would always insist they pick out the most beautiful and affluent perverts in the clubs. These were easily identifiable from their incredibly expensive latex outfits and fine, crafted leather accessories. With their guards down as they sought their decadent playtimes amongst some of the most sexually depraved individuals that society had to offer, the rich folk were like lambs to the slaughter. As an added bonus, they were also good to rob—their bank accounts were perpetually full and their credit cards bloated with high-interest credit, and this was how Richard provided for his expecting wife.

Claire stood in the dim, dank club next to her husband and lamented as to how far down the lavatory her life had gone since the day Karl had died his terrible, disgusting death, how she longed for the more innocent days when to her, scat was simply a type of free form jazz music.

She found herself standing by the unimaginatively named *piddling pool*, Claire barefoot in her ill-fitting black dress and Richard in blue latex shorts. Claire's dress, ass-height to start with, had ridden high on her pregnant belly and left her panty-less, neatly trimmed cunt fully exposed for all to enjoy. Her fat, swollen breasts bulged out of either side of the dress's top, and her taut nipples were clearly visible through the cheap material. A year ago, Claire wouldn't have been seen dead in public in a stripper dress such as that – although Karl would have her wear one on occasion in the bedroom, and they had even discussed installing a pole dancing pole in the spare room to complete their fantasy role play.

And just look how that had turned out.

"How about those two?" Richard pointed discretely to the couple who were romping in the piddling pool. The pool was actually nothing grander than a kiddie's inflatable paddling pool, which a group of five people—four men, one woman—were peeing into. The guys aimed their floppy dicks at the couple who were sloshing around and trying to have sex in the two-inch deep puddle of acrid urine whilst the lady amongst the pee-ers stretched open her labia and aimed her urethral opening the best she could; sadly, most of hers trickled down the inside of her thigh and soaked her bare feet.

Claire shook her head. The couple were easily early sixties, and, as low as her standards had dropped of late, she drew the line at wrinkled old flesh and floppy tits. And besides, whenever Richard fed from old people, it had a tendency to render him bad tempered and impotent.

Richard and Claire left the rancid pool and walked around the club; it was a busy night for sure, and the place was heaving with sweaty, dirty perverts, and the bare concrete floors were slick with bodily fluids of all descriptions. Richard made a beeline for the ominously labeled *vomitorium room.* He appeared to be not in the least bit interested in the slim, well-stacked blonde lady who was strapped to a wooden cross by the door. The blonde's husband was encouraging people to practice their fisting technique on his wife's already slack anus, and a small line had formed behind a petite redhead, whose hand was buried wrist-deep in the blonde's ass, whilst her shaven-headed girlfriend slurped at the lube/shit mix that bubbled out and dripped in long, shining strings onto the floor.

Claire followed her husband into the vomitorium and instantly recoiled at the pungent stink of bile, stomach acid, and somewhat inexplicably, tacos. Even after the events of the previous twelve months, and the disgusting things she had gotten used to, there was something about the stench of puke that still churned Claire's guts. Perhaps that was why Richard had selected this particular part of the club? He really could be a sadistic son of a bitch at times.

The room itself was small, no more than twenty feet square, and this added to the claustrophobic atmosphere and exacerbated the acidic tang that hung so thick in the air that Claire could almost reach out and touch it. The room was bare, windowless, and shared the same smooth, concrete floor as the rest of the club. Claire noted that the floor concaved slightly towards a metal grate in the center; most likely she was standing in what had once been one of the abattoir's killing rooms back in the day. This, she found to be disturbingly apt.

There were three couples already in the room when Richard led Claire in and closed the heavy metal door with a noisy clang behind them. Two of the couples had paired up and were busy smearing each other with slimy, yellow globs of puke; the stuff hung thick and lank in their hair, and their naked bodies glistened with it. One of the guys stuck three fingers in one of the women's mouths—it was impossible to tell who belonged to whom—and jabbed them down her throat. Instantly, she let out a gargled choke, and a fresh stream of vomit spurted out between his fingers and into his face. Their partnered couple licked at the mess as it slid down his neck and onto his chest.

The third couple in the room were dressed in matching tight leopard print latex cat suits that made their slim bodies look sleek and wet. They were just standing there and watching the sickly floorshow with a look of disgusted pleasure on their faces.

Richard made eye contact with Claire and nodded towards the leopard print couple. She acknowledged him with a forced smile, wordlessly letting him know that, yes, the couple would do nicely. Over and above her tolerance for the vile stench of Richard's grotesque predilections, she was most concerned at her new and nonchalant attitude towards the taking of lives.

Claire made her way across the room, her bare feet squishing in the cold, congealing puke that coated the floor, and her stomach churned as bits of regurgitated food stuck between her toes.

"Hi," she said to the latex-clad woman, "I'm Claire."

The woman turned around to face Claire, and her husband followed suit. At first, they appeared annoyed at having had their fun observing the other couples engaging in Roman showers interrupted, but, once their eyes roamed the length and breadth of Claire's magnificent body, their countenance cheered up some.

"I'm Rachel, and this is my husband, Roberto." The woman seemed unsure as to whether to shake Claire's hand or kiss her.

Claire made up the woman's mind for her and leaned in for a wet, open-mouthed smacker right on the lips. She wriggled her tongue inside Rachel's mouth and was greeted by the woman's reciprocating tongue.

"Richard," Richard introduced himself to Roberto above the background sounds of retching and puke spattering onto naked skin. He studied the man, and his good lady wife, who was busy tongue wresting with Claire, and saw that their faces were a little green, their outfits spotless save for the feet and sparse splashes of sick about the calves. They simply screamed newbies and were clearly in the process of working themselves up to trying out their fantasy of emetophillia for themselves.

Perfect.

Claire knew all too well that Richard so loved it when she played lesbian for him. So, she made a big show of seducing Rachel; get this right and she'd be guaranteed some quality sex from her husband after the inevitable conclusion of their evening's activities. Once he'd fed, that is. She pressed her lips tight to Rachel's, so much so that she could barely breathe, and she roamed her hands around the woman's tight, trim body. She kneaded Rachel's large, hemispherical breasts—disappointingly fake—and slapped her latex-clad buttocks so hard that the woman squealed into Claire's open mouth. Claire groped at her new lover's crotch and found to her delight, that the cat suit was fitted with a sturdy zipper running from pubic bone to lower back in order to expose the genitals at the appropriate moment. She unzipped and pushed her hand between Rachel's legs.

"Wait." Rachel broke the kiss and pushed Claire's hand away.

Claire looked at Rachel, then at Richard's disappointed face; how she hated that look from him, it never failed to make her feel so terribly small and insignificant.

"I want these." Rachel pulled aside the top of Claire's dress, and her twin engorged tits bounced free. Rachel took Claire's breasts in her hands and began massaging them. At first, she was extremely gentle as if Claire's tits were the most delicate of creatures, but, quickly, her urgency gathered, and she dug her fingers into the pliable flesh and squeezed hard.

All the while, Richard and Roberto looked on, and the couples in the background fucked each other noisily amidst their respective spilled stomach contents.

Claire moaned out loud, as she felt the merciful release in her swollen breasts, and a thick flow of creamy yellow colostrum oozed out of her nipples and snaked down the curve of each tit. She grabbed Rachel's hands and forced her to knead harder, increasing the flow.

Rachel leaned down and took a dribbling nipple into her mouth. She sucked it deep into the back of her throat like a feeding infant. At first, the viscous pre-milk tasted bitter and slimy and made her gag, but before long, she had grown used to it, and she gulped it down with aplomb.

Urged on by Richard, Roberto joined his wife at Claire's bosom and took the opposing nipple into his mouth. His cheeks hollowed as he sucked rigorously at the sticky fluid, and his Adam's apple bobbed up and down as he drank it down like it was the best thing he had ever tasted.

Claire actually enjoyed the sensation of the couple draining her teats like she was some fat, milking heifer; it nurtured both her sexual and maternal instincts and made her vagina so very wet and aching for Richard's fat, filling cock. Soon the colostrum—crammed with antibodies, so incredibly healthy—would give way to breast milk proper that would jet from the pores around her areolas in fine sprays of sweet liquid. Of that, Claire knew that the suckling couple wouldn't be able to get enough.

Richard looked on with an approving smile, his erection pushing out the front of his tight shorts in an impressive bulge that made an 'A' shape of his crotch. He glanced over at the other couples in the vomitorium and saw that it had become their turn to watch the impromptu floorshow, their own carnal appetites sated for the time being.

Having drunk more than their fill from Claire's profuse mammaries, Rachel and Roberto pulled away with great reluctance and a disappointed look on both their faces. Claire ran a finger around Roberto's mouth, tracing the contours of his thin lips whilst Richard did likewise with Rachel, his free hand stroking her hard nipples through the thin latex that stretched tightly over them.

With a sudden, aggressive motion, Claire slipped her finger inside Roberto's mouth and snaked it to the rear of his throat. There, she jabbed at that special spot that would activate the man's gag reflex. On cue, Roberto threw up his stomach full of rich breast milk in thick clots of yellow. He retched and heaved, and the rancid fluid poured over Claire's arm, down her breasts and spattered to the floor.

Rachel vomited the instant the offensively sour reek hit her nose, before Richard even had the opportunity to activate her gag reflex. Her own contribution to the rank mess spouted out through her nose before she had time to open her mouth and cascaded down Richard's chest. With an impish grin, Richard pulled open the waistband of his shorts to catch the jellied milk/bile mix. As his rubber shorts filled with Rachel's vomit, they ballooned out and a thin, watery yellow fluid trickled down along his thighs.

Lost in rapturous delight, Roberto and Rachel kissed and swapped the dregs of each other's vomitus between eager mouths whilst Claire scooped up handfuls of the stuff from her tits and fed it to them.

There were stifled retching sounds coming from the other couples in the room, and they shuffled by Claire and her companions, on their way to the door. The two women held their noses and coughed up clear, viscous mucus as they walked by with runny strings of come dripping from between their legs onto the puke-strewn floor; breast milk vomit play was clearly too much even for seasoned emetophiles.

Once they had gone, Richard slid the bolt that perched at the top of the metal door, locking him, Claire, and their new playthings inside the stinking room. With a smile at the couple, Richard slipped out of his shorts, and the coagulated throw up that had accumulated within slopped out and splashed around his feet. Then his body began to change.

Rachel and Roberto noticed nothing amiss, so wrapped up were they in each other they were totally oblivious as they kissed deeply and smeared each other's cat suits with the mess they had produced. Roberto's fingers were thrust between his partner's thighs and were playing frantically with her clitoris as she rubbed at his cock through his latex suit.

Claire stepped back from the couple, as Richard's body kind of *melted* and began to lose its shape. Those all too familiar fat, brown tendrils crawled out from his thighs, stomach, and crotch like malevolent snakes and made their way towards the unsuspecting couple.

The first either Rachel or Roberto knew what was happening was when Richard's fattest tendril snaked around Roberto's neck and jerked him backwards. Rachel yelped as the action forced her husband's jaws to snap shut, and he clamped his teeth down on her tongue, chomping away its tip.

"Bastard!" Rachel screamed, as blood poured down her chin.

Roberto was in no position to apologize as the oozing, pulsating thing Richard had become was strangling the life out of him. The glistening tendril wrapped tight around his neck to cut off the air to his aching lungs as his mouth gaped wide open and soundless, and his eyes bugged out as if attempting escape from their sockets. It was also evident that Roberto had shit himself; there was a large bulge in the rear of his cat suit that appeared to be making its way slowly and deliberately down the back of his legs.

Rachel staggered back and away from the

ghoulish thing Richard had transformed into. She gagged at the stench of defecation and death that effused from his amorphous frame and glanced across at Claire as if looking for help. There, she saw only empty detachment in the woman's eyes.

"Help him?" Rachel's voice was almost a whisper. "Please." She pressed her back against the vomitorium wall as a pair of Richard's pseudopods made their way through the clogs of vomit on the floor towards her.

Roberto's body fell limp but remained held upright by Richard. The tiny, sharp claws that sprouted from Richard's myriad tendrils had made short work of the latex cat suit, slicing it deftly away with rapid, deliberate movements. They had even chopped away the latex that covered the man's feet, so the fresh shit and accumulated sweat dribbled out in a slimy, putrid cocktail. The high-priced suit hung in shreds, which allowed yet more of Richard to penetrate Roberto's body and began the job of digesting it.

The slender tendrils Richard had sent towards the simpering Rachel grasped her wrists and pulled her towards where her husband was being broken down into a glutinous, bloodied mush.

"Please no!" Rachel cried out, as she was dragged towards Richard's oozing form. "You have to stop this!" she screamed at Claire.

As much as she wanted to, Claire couldn't tear her eyes away from the all-too familiar, gruesome scene, as Richard welcomed Rachel's struggling body into his; as much as she needed to close her eyes to the terrible fate that the couple were experiencing, a perverse part of Claire figured she owed them at least enough to force herself to bear witness to their demise.

Richard wriggled a thick, phallic tendril up into Rachel's vagina, then another into her ass, and she screamed out in pain. A wide, membranous flap of

Richard's flesh grew out from his back like a giant, perverse bat's wing and he wrapped it around Rachel, and all that Claire could see was the poor woman's tear-streamed face.

"You can stop this!" Rachel implored, a sad look of resignation across her face. "It's only a fecal spirit! At least stop it before it gets your baby!"

Claire looked quizzically at the woman.

Richard clamped a clump of his shit-flesh that was still roughly hand shaped over Rachel's mouth and pulled her into his body, absorbing her flesh quickly and efficiently as she dissolved.

Rachel bit down on the smothering hand and chewed away a gobbet of the foul-tasting stuff. Richard recoiled slightly, and Rachel spat out her mouthful. "Look in the fucking onion!" She screamed, and blood and shit sprayed from her mouth, and her head vanished inside the brown, seething bulk of Richard's body.

"I wouldn't if I were you, darling," Richard said, as, once again, he began to take on a more human shape, and Claire thought he'd never sounded more like Russell Brand.

ELEVEN

Richard was out again. He'd called an Uber almost the minute he'd woken up that morning and headed out shortly thereafter. Claire knew that his hasty departure and hired ride could only mean one thing—Richard intended to come home steaming drunk and stinking of cheap whores again. It wasn't as if he hadn't fed sufficiently at the scat club the previous night—the unfortunate Rachel and Roberto would have provided Richard with more than enough sustenance to keep him going for at least a month, maybe longer. The only conclusion Claire could draw was that her husband was going out to get away from her and to experience the thrill of the hunt, anonymous clandestine fucking and the fun of the kill. She doubted very much that her husband would feed on whomever that day's unsuspecting victim would be—man or woman, he really had no preference—to do so would mean getting fat, and Richard's over inflated ego simply wouldn't tolerate that.

And it wasn't as if Claire had not satisfied him sexually after he'd finished feeding; as usual, Richard was horny as hell after his two-course meal, and Claire had taken full advantage of that, to sate her own carnal needs. She'd fucked him good and hard, as they sprawled amongst the puke, blood, and the shit-stains in that cold, desolate room, Richard's fat penile protrusions filling her cunt, ass and mouth all at the same time. Claire and Richard had come together—his timing was always impeccable in that respect—and then they'd snuck out of the club, through a fire door, into a moss-lined alleyway at the back.

Save for the blood stains and bits of shredded latex from Rachel and Roberto's cat suits, no one would ever have suspected foul play in the vomitorium; torn clothing and blood was pretty much par for the course in such establishments. Nor would anyone at the club notice that the couple was missing, those places rarely took names, and on the odd occasion that they did, the ones they were given were invariably false. Therefore, it would be days before anyone noticed the delectable Rachel and Roberto missing, and forever before they were traced to the scat club - it was hardly the kind of place you tell your family and friends about.

Such was the Richards' all-too familiar pattern, hence Richard's penchant for the underground club scene; there was safety in the anonymity that they afforded a creature such as him.

A *fecal spirit*?

Claire was positive that was the phrase Rachel had screamed at her just before Richard dissolved the life out of her lithe body. It was something Claire hadn't heard before, especially in reference to her husband. But at the very least the term in itself had made some sense.

...before it gets your baby!

This, too, had echoed around inside Claire's brain since Rachel had yelled it out as her swansong; it had bounced around in Claire's maternal mind and had kept her awake all night. It had made her uncharacteristically antsy for Richard to leave the trailer, so she could be alone to do a little research, a fact that she hoped she'd hidden well from him.

Usually, on the times that Richard chose to go out by himself—which had become ever more frequent as her pregnancy wore on—it would break off a little piece of Claire's heart, and more often than not, she would cry to herself and eat chocolate. But today Richard's predictable behavior had suited her, despite the insidious thoughts of his screwing someone else that gnawed away at the back of her mind like some malignant disease.

Claire flipped open her laptop's lid and thumbed the grubby *on* switch. The computer whirred to life, and the screen blazed with her old company logo - a stark reminder of more affluent, fulfilling and happier times.

Once the thing booted up—it seemed to take it an age these days—Claire Googled 'fecal spirit' and drew a complete blank. She even tried the UK spelling with the 'a' added—but still nothing. Frustrated, Claire buried her face in her hands. Richard wouldn't be gone all day. She only had a short window of opportunity to do this before he returned.

Look in the onion.

The final words of a dying woman, cryptic, yet somehow, they rang the faintest of bells in the dusty recesses of Claire's brain.

"Of course!" She exclaimed and actually slapped her forehead with the heel of her hand—like they do in the dumb sitcoms to denote when a character has had a revelation of the obvious.

Claire had come across this before, back when her company had been developing anonymity software; the Onion was the gateway to the Deep Web - those dark recesses of the Internet in which skulked the very worst of the human under class. Amongst those lurking in the murkiest shadows of cyberspace were individuals whose perversions were too twisted, even for the extremes of the readily available internet: the pedophiles, drug dealers, Devil worshippers, terrorists, serial killers and much, much worse. That the answers to Claire's questions about the thing that she'd married would reside there filled her with more dread than she thought possible, even for someone who lived with a murderous being formed from her own wastes.

She couldn't help but chastise herself for not having done this before. How come she hadn't thought to question her husband? Most likely because the way things had so spectacularly imploded around her at the time – Karl's infidelity and gruesome death, the attempted kidnap, her company's collapse, Richard's arrival – she had been more than willing to have something – *anything* – to cling on to. Why would she question the one thing that had been there for her, the one thing that had provided at least a little stability?

It took but a few minutes to download and install the necessary software and before long, Claire was delving into the darkest depths of the internet.

***

Richard was delighted when the woman invited him back to her place. He'd picked her up in a hipster coffee bar in town, a place well known for the bored housewives from the gated estates who used it for casual hook-ups. She had approached him as he sat in his usual spot by the window, reading the complimentary Wall Street Journal; he'd not even had to go through the rigmarole of buying her a cappuccino.

He was less than delighted, however, when she drove him out of town to a dilapidated industrial zone, not too far from the abattoir scat club where he'd eaten the night before and told him that she liked her casual sex rough and dirty and out in the open.

"I want you to fuck me here," the woman said—Richard still hadn't asked her name, didn't give enough of a shit—and she unzipped her expensive dress and folded it neatly onto the front seat of her Mercedes. She unhooked her bra and unveiled a splendid pair of natural breasts, both of which were pierced through their gloriously pink, swollen nipples and sported gold hoops adorned with a solitary diamond each. She kicked off her shoes, slipped off her lacy thong and stood naked in a muddy puddle in the narrow alleyway between two abandoned, crumbling factory units.

"Here?" Richard looked around nervously, expecting to see a security guard at any moment. "Sure you don't want to fuck in the car?"

"I'm not a motherfucking teenager." The woman sounded impatient. "You want some of this pussy, or not?" She pulled her denuded labia apart to give Richard a most delectable flash of raw, wet pink.

"Yes, Ma'am." Richard smiled and unzipped his pants.

The woman knelt down in the puddle and smeared its oily mud over her body in the interests of putting on a show for Richard. She grinded the filth into her firm buttocks and tits and wiped it across her face.

"I'm your filthy whore now," she purred

"Do whatever you want to my disgusting, cheap body."

Richard smiled a knowing smile, *if only she knew*.

She lay on her back in the wet and spread her legs wide apart, and Richard could see that she was glistening wet and aroused, and he couldn't make up his mind whether he should fuck her before or after he killed her.

"Wow," the woman gasped as Richard unveiled his magnificent dick. It hung there before her, fat and heavy between his thighs, with its purple head swollen and glinting in the sunlight that reflected off of the broken factory windows opposite.

"Are you going to fuck my wet cunt with that, big boy?"

Richard acquiesced and knelt down between the woman's legs; the puddle cold on his bare knees. He aimed his dick with one hand, steadied himself against the wall with the other, and in the blink of an eye, he was inside her.

The woman squealed her pleasure at the top of her lungs as Richard's cock filled her up, and she rubbed more of the foul mud onto her breasts. "Fuck me hard!" she screamed. "Make me dirty, you fucker!"

Richard looked around again, paranoid that his date's loud exclamations would attract unwanted attention; the last thing he needed right now was to be arrested. This was supposed to have been a for-fun fuck, and it was becoming more onerous by the minute.

"Oh my god!" the woman screamed and pulled at her black-dyed hair. "You are so fucking *big*!" Her voice bounced around the abandoned buildings and scared a sparse flock of mangy pigeons into flight.

Richard punched the woman square in the face, and suddenly she was reassuringly quiet. He'd felt the cartilage in her nose crunch beneath his knuckles and her front teeth knock free of her gums. A splash of bright crimson decorated her grimy face, and she made a peculiar gurgling noise in the back of her throat, as the blood from her shattered nose made its way towards her lungs.

Richard humped away at the woman's flaccid, mud-soaked body until he came, as he wasn't about to let the fact that she was unconscious and drowning in her own blood put him off his hard-earned release. As Richard fucked the woman, he encircled his powerful hands around her neck and strangled the life from her.

Once that formality was over and done with, Richard rifled through the dead woman's purse and car for money, credit cards and anything else of value.

Stepping back to take stock of the muddied corpse in the puddle with its filth smeared tits, legs spread wide and the thick cream of his ejaculate dribbling from her vagina, Richard fought the urge to feed. He could see that she had soiled herself as she'd died—he'd actually felt the warm flood of her piss on his balls at the moment of death—and the sight of the half-solid turd moulded into the cleft of her ass crack was making him feel quite esurient.

Richard's dick, far from deflating after being spent, had continued its expansion until it hung so low between his legs as to scrape on the rough asphalt that had once been the factory's parking lot. He could feel his body begin to soften from its human form, his flesh becoming pliable and reeking of waste and his dick wriggled towards the woman with what seemed to be a life of its own. Richard had no choice but to follow its lead, and like an alcoholic unable to walk past a bar's welcoming neon sign and heady aroma of beer and smoke, he fell upon the warm, fleshy corpse and began to feed.

***

Claire was having trouble believing what she was seeing. She'd searched for 'fecal spirit' within the realms of the Deep Web, and whilst part of her had wished she'd never begun her endeavor, another part—a big one—was telling her she really ought to have done so much sooner. Although, what would she have researched? She'd only just heard the term *fecal spirit,* and whilst Richard had proven himself to be just another shithead guy who treated her like dirt, she'd had no reason to suspect he may have had an ulterior motive when it came to her unborn child.

Whilst there had been no shortage of scat fetish sites on the regular parts of the internet—such proclivities may be abhorrent to the masses, but, as with any fetish, there was definitely something for everyone—hidden within the virtual shadows of the Deep Web there were those who took the whole thing to the extreme.

In those darkest of the dark places, Claire discovered an entire underground network of sick, perverted people who dedicated their lives to the worship of human waste, and shit seemed to hold the most reverence. To these people, excrement was their god, and it was believed to hold some almost divine powers, having been '*born of man*'.

These weird people had their own societies and clubs—far deeper underground and more exclusive than any that Claire had ever visited—in which participants were willing sacrifices in the myriad attempts to invoke what were most commonly referred to as the *fecal spirits*.

Claire followed a link that was written in a dark purple, which made it difficult to read on her laptop screen. There, she discovered a bizarre underground movement (ha!) in amongst the run-of-the-mill

Satanists and other creepy cults that seemed to be mostly dedicated to perverse sexual practices and ritualized murder.

The Unholy Church of the Fecal Spirits welcomes you.

It read:
We believe in the invocation and nurturing of these most wonderful and ephemeral of all the Earth Spirits; cast below ground with the waste of the humans that created them, they yearn to feel the sunlight on their flesh, the earth's sweet air inside their bodies.

So far, so hippy bullshit, Claire thought. She scrolled down.

Our mission is to bring substance and life to our fellow spirits and to give them the freedom that we—their discarders—*take so very much for granted. This, we achieve by worship at the Holy Temple of the Human bowel and the practical impregnation of willing followers.*

Claire shuddered; she had never seen herself as a willing anything, she'd simply gotten hopelessly drunk and let a complete stranger fuck her in the ass.

She scrolled down a little more, her interest in the flowery hippy-speak waning fast; she was looking for answers to who—*what*—her husband was and not a cack-handed attempt at indoctrination into some freakish cult.

Another link led to a simple white text on black background page entitled *The Spirits,* and it was there that Claire found what she had been looking for; something that chilled her down to her very core.

Once our Fecal Spirit brethren have been given life, to achieve their permanent form they must partake of an infant born of their own mother, whom is to be assimilated along with said mother, so they can each take pleasure in eternity as one within one.

And there it was.

Claire could feel the cold chill of fear creep up along her spine like some freakish invertebrate and a startling clarity of mind that she had not experienced in well over a year.

The poor, doomed woman at the scat club had been trying to warn her, even as she surely knew her own fate at Richard's hands. *Perhaps*, the thought struck Claire, *she had been a mother herself, and her concern over Claire's baby had been an unconsciously maternal one*. And *that* thought set off a chain reaction of guilt and pain that attacked Claire's conscience like a malignant, growing thing.

The woman—Rachel—had clearly known more about Richard and his type than Claire had. Obviously, she hadn't been as much the Newbie as she and Richard had assumed; Rachel's warning was for the life of Claire's unborn child - and Claire's as its mother. Claire very much doubted that Rachel would have shown her as much concern had she not been with child, given the circumstances of their acquaintance.

"Dear, sweet Jesus," Claire whispered beneath her breath, as she forced herself to continue reading down the dark black of the page. Further down, the pseudo-religious composition continued on, and explained, in its round about, poetic fashion, that when a fecal spirit feeds upon the freshly born child of the woman that spawned it, it was called *rebirthing,* and once that had been achieved, the spirit could then go on to impregnate other human beings with its shitty little offspring.

...and they who do so shall walk the earth forever in immortality, which only those who gave life to their fecal offspring can undo.

As with all things of such ilk, there were rules. There would always be rules, as there are in real life; just like the female mosquito who must feed on blood before her eggs can become fertile—a rule that the species has no choice but to adhere to in order to procreate. It was likewise with Richard and his kind. They had to wait for their victim to be born before feeding upon it, and then they would duly dispatch the mother in order to prevent harm coming to the spirit that created them. And it was often those same rules that were their undoing, much as the mosquito could so easily be crushed out of existence with a swift slap of a hand.

So that was how come Richard was hanging around Claire like a bad smell. She was nothing more now to him than a vessel for his own immortality, an occasional plaything, and the means by which to entice the innocent people who became his nourishment.

Unfortunately, being used came naturally to Claire. Karl had done it successfully for the two years prior to his departure and Richard's arrival, and now Richard was doing pretty much the same to her. The main difference was that Karl was only after her money, and not her baby and her life.

With an anxious glance at the door, Claire reluctantly scrolled down to the bottom of the web page. There, she saw a handful of thumbnail pictures that the blurb promised showed the stages of a rebirth. She clicked on the first image, and it filled her screen in vivid Technicolor; a monstrous, amorphous blob of what was quite clearly excrement was sucking the life from a small baby with its grotesque tendrils, the baby's head already hollowed out like some macabre breadbasket. The child was so fresh that its umbilicus was still attached to its round belly and snaked the short way across the floor to disappear up into its mother's vagina. Standing around the monstrous scene were a half dozen people with their faces uplifted as if in prayer, each one of them stark naked and smeared in lumpy, brown clumps of poop.

Claire threw up in her mouth a little and clicked the cross in the top right of the image. She selected the last of the thumbnails, as she had no desire to see the disgusting progression of the baby's digestion by the shapeless creature or the inevitable death of its mother.

And there he was.

In all his nude glory was the mysterious guy Claire had fucked so wantonly, so *willingly* after the conference. He was smiling into the camera, his body fully formed and so incredibly human, yet still with that faint waxy sheen that had become so familiar to Claire. His body was completely hairless and incredibly muscular in the way his biceps, abs, quads and calves bulged and rippled. His broad, bare feet stood in the bloodstain that was all that remained of the infant and its mother, and it seemed as though he were staring directly into Claire's soul. The man's eyes sparkled with a remarkable intensity; his smile was white and broad and brought back to Claire the vivid memory of the debauched night they'd spent together.

There was the man—the *fecal spirit*—who had burdened her with Richard, who had set off a chain of events that would ultimately lead to her death, the death of her child, and innumerable others, once Richard rebirthed. Claire allowed herself a wry smile, despite her horror and revulsion. There on the web page before her was the only person—*thing*—that could put a stop to Richard.

And all she had to do was find him.

TWELVE

Claire almost turned back twice, once because she had a terrible realization that she was acting solely upon what she'd read on some shady web site, and again because she wasn't convinced that Ethan Foote actually lived in such a crappy part of town.

She pulled up outside a rundown shotgun shack that cowered in between a pair of hideous, utilitarian apartment buildings. On the sidewalk, a gang of grubby faced kids, who ought really to have been in school, were playing with a roadkill armadillo. They were gleefully poking at the flattened thing with sticks, as if trying to force the thing back to life, even though most of its innards had squirted out through its ass and lay caked and drying on the blacktop. On the opposite side of the neglected, potholed road, there skulked a small pack of dogs, and they eyed the kid's plaything with jealous, hungry eyes.

Claire walked the short way to the front door of Ethan's home under the watchful eyes of both the kids and the dogs. She knocked.

The door cracked open a little, and the unmistakable, broad shape of Ethan Foote's head poked out. In the background, Claire could make out a handful of small children scurrying about.

"Miss Jepson?" Foote looked puzzled; he'd not so much as laid eyes on his ex-boss since the day she'd told him that the company was closing, and he no longer had gainful employment. As things had transpired, that had actually been the last day he'd worked.

"Who is it?" A woman's harpy voice trilled from behind the big man. "If they've come about the car you can tell 'em we'll pay 'em when we can, and they can fuck off!"

"It's Miss Jepson." Foote called back into the gloomy hovel. "From work."

"That bitch?" the harsh voice replied. "You can tell her that she can fuck off, as well!"

Claire offered Foote a wry smile; this was hardly the language one would have expected from the erstwhile Captain of the high school Debate Club.

"Sorry about that." Foote grinned to hide his embarrassment. He stepped out from the doorway and eased the door closed behind him. "It's good to see you," he said.

It was Claire's turn to be embarrassed. The last time they'd been together, she had been dressed to kill in a designer suit and had still been his boss. Now, she just looked disheveled, poor, and grotesquely pregnant in a knee length denim skirt and a loose-fitting hooded top. "I need your help, Ethan," she told him. "I really didn't know who else to turn to."

Foote towered over Claire, his wide, moon face a picture of concern. "Sure thing." He smiled. "What's the problem?"

"If it's okay with you, I can explain everything in the

car." She nodded towards the battered old Camry, around which the feral kids had gathered, painfully aware that it was a world away from the gleaming Aston Martin she used to drive. "We need to get going straight away."

"Going where?"

"New Orleans," Claire told him. "I have some trouble I need to get sorted out."

Foote, as always, was unflinching in his loyalty to Claire, unquestioning of anything she asked of him, even though he was no longer in her employ. "Give me five," he said.

Claire walked back to her car, as Foote disappeared back inside his home. She could hear shouting and kids crying and something that sounded awfully like things being thrown, and part of her began to regret imposing on her old friend this way. But then, she reminded herself, she really did have no one else to turn to, and she needed someone who would believe her story, no matter how absurd it sounded, and help her to sort out the shit storm she had gotten herself into.

"I'll be back when I'm back!" Ethan appeared back at the door with a battered blue Adidas sports bag, bulging with what Claire assumed would be spare clothes.

"Don't fucking bother, you useless *cunt*!" Ethan's good lady wife followed him and stood on the threshold of their home with a grizzling infant clutched to her hip and a fat spliff dangling from the corner of her snarling mouth.

Claire offered a feeble wave from the sanctuary of her car and was damned if she couldn't remember the woman's name.

Foote pulled open the car door, slung his bag on to the back seat, and squeezed his immense frame into the shotgun seat.

"I'm sorry about-" Claire began.

"Don't be," Foote interrupted with a cheeky wink. "She'll be alright. Probably do us some good to have a little time apart, don't ya think?" His broad chest heaved with what could have been either a laugh or a sob or a mixture of both, and he pulled on his seat belt. "Now, then, I think you should tell me what you're getting me into this time."

Claire smiled at him, and for the first time in a long time she felt just a tad more secure. She gunned the engine and pulled away from the curb, scattering the gaggle of kids who ran after her as she drove away. They waved their sticks high in the air in an imaginary victory salute, and they reminded Claire of the child soldiers she'd seen on documentaries about the deepest, most unpleasant corners of war-torn Africa.

It was fortuitous that Claire and Ethan were facing a six-hour drive; she certainly did have some explaining to do.

***

Detective Howgard was on her way into a meeting when the alert went off on her iPhone; a high-pitched trilling sound that sounded like something alien.

"For fuck's sake," she grumbled and dug the offending device from her pocket. She pressed the touch screen over the icon for her GPS app.

Eyes glued to the phone, Howgard took a quick detour into the restroom and locked herself into one of the empty stalls. In the adjacent stall, somebody was having a spectacularly bad time of things, and from the foul stink permeating from within, Howgard guessed that Thai food had something to do with it. The smell didn't bother Howgard too much, never had; she'd been brought up downwind of a water treatment plant, and on a bad day, everything around her neighborhood would stink of decaying human excrement. Little did the detective know just how useful her built-in tolerance to the pong would become.

The alert had been from the geofence she had programmed in for the tracking unit she'd secreted on the Jepson-Richards' car, and it could only mean one thing; either Mr. or Mrs. Jepson-Richards—or possibly both—were leaving town.

"Motherfucker," Howgard cursed beneath her breath. "I fucking *knew* it."

"Is that you, Skyler?" a disembodied voice came over from the next stall. It was followed by a pained grunt and a faint *splish-splash* noise.

"Yep," Howgard confessed.

"Cool, can you let the boss know I'll be late for the meeting?"

"Sure thing," Howgard replied, as she bustled from her stall. Of course, she had more pressing things to attend to; Sergeant Pizano's meeting was just going to have to wait.

***

Richard staggered into the trailer sometime after the bars closed. He reeked of cheap liquor and had a hard-on that demanded urgent attention. He felt fat, bloated and helplessly lethargic on account of the booze, and the rich woman he'd fed on earlier. Even so, he had that insatiable itch that required scratching.

"Honey, I'm home!" he called out into the dark trailer with a chuckle. He fumbled for the light switch and flicked on the fluorescent tube that flickered and hummed to life above his head. "Where the fuck are you, my *darling*?" he slurred in that inimitable accent of his. "In bed already, you lazy bitch?" He stumbled towards the bedroom and tugged at his belt. He slid his pants and underwear down his firm thighs and kicked them off. He stroked his formidable dick with both hands, and it grew even harder in his hand.

Claire was not in their bed. Nor was she hiding in the miniscule bathroom, as she often did when he came home in this state of inebriation. Richard began to feel the anger welling up inside him, could sense the essence of his true being beginning to bubble and rise up in his craw, ready to let loose his immense displeasure.

He retrieved his pants from across the room, fished out his cell phone, and thumbed Claire's number on his contacts list. He listened intently as her phone rang out and suddenly went through to her voice mail; she'd clearly dummied him, and that did nothing to appease his temper.

It was then that Richard spied Claire's laptop on the table. He powered it up and flicked through her Internet search history. Saw nothing there that concerned him, nothing to indicate why she would have just upped and left, or where she had gone.

Then he saw the onion icon on the desktop, it stood out immediately as something new—Claire was nothing if not a creature of habit, and she'd not added a single thing to her computer in the entire year Richard had known her. Richard double clicked on the image, and the web page it threw up on the screen made him recoil in horror.

"Bitch," Richard growled, as he swallowed down the panic that left its acid burn at the back of his throat. He dialed the Uber number on his cell phone and booked himself another ride.

THIRTEEN

Claire had made good time in the first four hours of their journey, with only three restroom stops, the bane of a pregnant woman and her decreasing bladder capacity. Her ankles had swollen up like party balloons, too, and she had a kink in her hip that was the Devil's own business.

As she drove, Claire's one-time security guard/booty call had listened intently as she regaled him with tales of talking, killer poop, excrement made human, the unpleasant undoing of her fiancé, the downfall of Jepson Software Solutions, and of course, Richard Richards. Foote had given every impression of having taken the whole incredible story rather well, with only a sage nod of the head or the occasional raised eyebrow to punctuate what Claire was telling him.

But did he actually *believe* what he was hearing? Or did he merely believe that she believed it? If so, he must be thinking her quite insane by now.

"There you have it, warts and all," Claire declared

upon finishing her yarn spinning. "I know it's a big ask that you believe me…"

"He gave you warts as well?" Foote broke his silence.

Claire sighed. Perhaps it had been a mistake to bring the big dork along after all; he may have the brawn, but he was still as thick as pig shit.

"Gotcha!" Foote split a broad grin and gave Claire a wink. He laughed out loud, his voice big and booming within the confines of the car. Claire slapped his thick, solid arm and allowed herself to laugh along with him, more with relief than actual mirth.

"Bastard," she growled.

"Of course, I believe you," Foote reassured. "I mean, it's hardly something you could make up, is it?" He glanced across at her. "I've known you a long time, Claire, and you've never been blessed with an active imagination." He smiled at her again.

Claire frowned at Foote, but her indignation at his slight against her creativity melted at the smile, and all at once, they were back in high school, and she was all weak at the knees at the Ethan Foote who was all masculine hormones and sour sweat in his football gear.

"Thank you," she said. "I think."

"Anytime."

"And thank you for agreeing to come along with me. All this must seem crazy to you."

"My pleasure, Ma'am." Foote nodded. "And, yep, it sure does that." He patted Claire's knee, physical contact to emphasize solidarity. Sure, the whole thing did seem like an incredibly tall tale, but it certainly fit in with the unholy mess that he'd been faced with in the boardroom that day, plus the disappearance of the three board members and the detective. To Foote, living shit was as good an explanation as any right now. "Only question is: what the fuck do we do about it all?"

Claire gave her companion a look, as her knee tingled where he'd touched her, not unlike the static prickle one receives from walking on cheap nylon carpet. "That's what I'm hoping we can find out in New Orleans," she said. "We just need to find the guy who impregnated me with Richard." She stroked her bulging belly. "If *impregnated* is the right word for what that cocksucker did to me."

"And if we don't?"

"Then I guess I'll just have to keep on running," Claire said with sadness in her voice. She knew full well that Richard would follow her wherever she went, that he always would until he achieved his objective of feeding on her unborn child.

Only this time around, it suited her purpose that he give chase - it was why she'd left such an obvious clue on her laptop. She needed him there when—*if*—she tracked down her post-conference guy, so he could do what ever needed to be done to revoke Richard's fecal spirit. In that respect, Richard would be walking straight into her cunning trap. However, if she failed to find her guy, then her only other recourse would be to keep on moving and hope that Richard would never catch up.

Only, she knew in her heart that he would. Richard knew her mind all too intimately and would always be hot on her heels.

"I'm going to pull over at the next rest stop, Ethan," Claire said. "I'll let you drive the last leg, and I need to…you know."

"Anything you say, Ma'am." Foote grinned that broad grin of his, and Claire felt the static tingle creep up between her legs and settle there.

***

Richard was less than an hour and a half behind his wife, his Uber driver having insisted on adhering to every speed limit, despite practically every other driver on the I-10 overtaking them.

"Can't be too careful these days, there's loads of traffic cops in unmarked vehicles," he told Richard, pronouncing the latter word *veee-hikals*, which did nothing to curb Richard's irritation.

"Could we pull over soon?" Richard remained outwardly polite; he'd fielded the 'what part of London are you from?' questions and listened to the driver's dreary life story for the past few hours and what he really needed was for the man's voice to shut the fuck up now.

"Could do with a rest room break myself," the man said with a cheer in his tone. "Think I'll treat myself to one of those gas station coffees while we're there."

Richard's Uber driver—Mike, Mick, or some such—never did get that coffee.

He pulled off of the highway and into a gas station that was seemingly in the middle of nowhere. There was a huge billboard advertising a 'gator farm nine miles on and very little else. Richard had him park the car at the farthest point from the gas station—told him he needed the walk to stretch his legs and avoid deep vein thrombosis—and the instant the car was in park, Richard had clamped a hand on the top of the man's head.

Richard's hand dissolved in to its natural pliable constituency and flowed quickly downwards to cover the driver's entire head, stifling the scream that formed in the unfortunate man's throat, as his head began to dissolve under Richard's grip.

In no time at all, Mike (Mick, Mac?) quit twitching and jerking, and his head collapsed in on itself, as Richard absorbed hair, flesh, bone, and brains up through his hand.

And in less than five minutes, there was nothing left of the Uber driver, save an unpleasant looking stain on the driver's seat.

Richard clambered over from the back seat and made himself comfortable behind the steering wheel; he had to scoot the seat back almost to its limit because the driver had apparently had unfeasibly stumpy legs. Annoyed that he'd added yet more to his own weight, yet pleased to be rid of the incessant, inane chatter, Richard threw the car into *D* and pulled back onto the highway.

***

Claire left the rest stop bathroom with a great sense of relief at having voided the bladder that her baby had been using as a punching bag. She was also feeling decidedly horny, so much so that she had eschewed putting her panties back on and was enjoying the warm breeze that wafted up her sensible length skirt and over her damp pussy.

Foote was across the way studying the vending machines, deliberating for what seemed an age between a Snickers bar and Cheesy Doritos, as Claire strode with purpose towards him. She grabbed his hand and led him in silence back to her Camry, which was parked in the almost deserted lot.

The sex they had together was animalistic and urgent. Claire bundled Foote into the back seat and climbed in after him. She hiked up her skirt and fumbled around with his pants until he was forced to take charge and unbuckle them to free his swelling cock. He'd begun to guide its hot, moist tip towards her ass—just like old times—but she took it from him with one trembling hand and crammed it into her aching vagina.

"I want it in there," she whispered. "Now, fuck me."

And fuck her he did, and they had incredibly hard, fast, sweaty sex, and Claire groaned out loud, as she grated her clit against Foote's pubic bone. She relished the almost forgotten sensation of regular, good ol' vanilla sex; it had been far too long.

Then it was done, over. Claire muffled the cry that had built up within her with her hand, her shriek still piercing against the salt-sweat of her palm. Foote grunted like some primeval creature—the only sound he *ever* made when fucking—and came inside Claire with great, shuddering spasms.

Sated, Claire rested her fat, pregnant body against Foote's heaving chest a while to get her breath back. It felt good to be so close to another human being, she was amazed as to just how *real* it felt and realized just how much she'd missed it.

"We should get going," Claire broke the stilted silence between them. "It'll be dark before we get there as it is."

It was with a great reluctance that they disentangled and rearranged their clothing in order to leave the confines of the Camry's back seat. Once settled in the front seats and back on their way—Foote driving, as he'd promised her—Claire put her time to good use researching on her phone the most likely places to find what they were looking for; looking for anywhere that rang even the faintest bell in her foggy memories of that fateful night a year ago.

As they hit the highway and continued on East, Claire began to wish she'd not left her panties back at the rest stop; Foote's semen was oozing out from her vagina at a most plenteous rate—she'd forgotten just how much of the stuff he could produce. It trickled down between her legs, pooling beneath her thighs as gravity guided it there, and she feared it would leave one hell of a stain on the seat.

FOURTEEN

They arrived in New Orleans' French Quarter just as the clear blue sky was giving way to the gray and salmon pink of dusk. It was less than a week before the clocks were due to jump back from daylight savings so nightfall tended to come around five thirty-six.

"We can find a hotel later," Claire said, as Foote squeezed the car trunk-first into a tight spot between a bright yellow Hummer and an F250 in the multi-storey; the Toyota looked dwarfed, like a kid's *Hot Wheels* toy. What she had to stop herself from voicing was that if this excursion failed to go as planned, they wouldn't need a hotel for the night; they'd either be running for their lives, or quite possibly have suffered a fate far worse.

"Happy to sleep in the car if we have to," Foote grumbled, although the very thought of him cramping his massive frame to sleep in anything less than a mini van was ludicrous.

"We should make a start." Claire brought up the

map app on her cell, and her face lit up with its cold light. "I guess we should start on Bourbon Street. It's where most things kick off in New Orleans." She had the vaguest of recollections of the night after the conference, of jazz music and strip joints and milling crowds of drunken people swigging vile colored drinks from plastic receptacles. And the smell, that heady, almost otherworldly aroma of vomit and stale piss. It was feeble, but it was all she had to go on, and all she could hope for was that something would jolt her memory and point her in the right direction.

Foote struggled out of his side of the Camry. He had to suck in his belly in order to squeeze out between the tightly packed vehicles. He knocked the door mirror off of the Hummer with his shoulder, and there was a loud crack, as its plastic casing crumpled beneath his weight. Foote winced and gave Claire a sheepish grin, as he caught the busted mirror and laid it, dangling by its tangle of wires, against the car's door like a dog's ripped ear.

"Oops." His voice was quiet.

Claire fared only slightly better in exiting the Camry. She managed to only just manoeuver her rotund abdomen between her car and the truck, and thankfully, the F250 remained intact when she was free. She popped the trunk and fished out an old pair of maternity jeans and a pair of utilitarian panties; her denim skirt was still damp from her romp with Foote, and somehow wearing a skirt and knowing what she was likely to be facing made her feel a little vulnerable. Unsure as to why she felt the need to preserve her modesty in front of Foote, Claire slipped the panties and jeans on under her skirt and *then* hiked down the skirt and stepped out of it.

"It's this way." She pointed out towards the city with a vague wave of the hand and waddled towards the exit stairwell.

Claire and Foote walked for a half hour along Canal

Street, more or less following the throng of revelers who were out for a good time in the heart of the Big Easy. Then, they hit upon Bourbon Street. Claire took a right, Foote close behind, and they were suddenly shoulder-to-shoulder with a mass of drunk, laughing people amid the garish glow of countless neon lights and the nauseating stink of revelry.

Claire pushed Foote in front of herself to take advantage of his broad frame, in order to manoeuver through the crowd. All the while, she was desperately looking for something, *anything* that would jog her nebulous memory.

"There." She grabbed Foote's arm and spun him around with such ferocity that he actually yelped. "That's where the Indian restaurant was. I remember the tattoo parlor next to it." A vivid flash in her memory let her know that, whilst she was looking in the right place, the Indian restaurant where her mystery man had wined and dined her was now a less than salubrious place selling gyros, pizza and a mind-boggling array of daiquiris.

Fighting with determination against the flow of people, Claire made her way to the vendor of the new store. There, she asked if they knew what had happened to the Indian eatery that had once stood on that very spot.

"Closed down almost a year ago, went bust," the gyro seller told her. "Folk want jambalaya and etouffee on Bourbon Street, not whatever that disgusting stuff was they were selling." He offered Foote a toothy grin. "You gonna buy a drink for the lady?"

"We're looking for a club," Foote countered, as he towered over the painfully thin, black guy. "A *special* kind of club."

"Ah, I understand." The man shot a sly wink at

Claire. "Then I would recommend the place across the street, that's very special, if you get ma' meaning." He pointed at a strip joint that gave an illicit promise of *almost* underage girls within. Although, the questionable bikini-clad individuals at the door who had the job of enticing customers seemed to be well beyond legal age—even from where she was standing, Claire could see their stretch marks and C-section scars.

"I have discount vouchers, half price entry for the lady. Tell 'em Marcel sent you."

"Not that kind of special," Claire butted in. "There's a place somewhere around here that caters for *particular* tastes." She tried to get her point across without being too vulgar—or cryptic. "I think it's near a voodoo store."

"Can't help you there, Ma'am." Marcel shrugged his weedy shoulders. "There's a whole shitload of voodoo stores here—this is New Orleans, you know." His amiable grin slipped a little. "Now, are you gonna buy something or not?"

Slurping on her thick, green daiquiri that tasted vaguely of watermelon and sugar, Claire wandered the full length of Bourbon Street behind Foote. She grew ever more despondent by the minute, peering down every side street, every alleyway, taking in every blast of Dixieland jazz music and whiff of stale beer that wafted out from the cool doorways, and still saw nothing that triggered her memory.

"I think we should go eat," Foote said on their second trip back along the street. "You look like you could do with sitting awhile."

Claire was forced to admit that her companion was right; her stomach was growling like some pissed off bear. Her legs ached, and her back hurt like hell from lugging the weight of her belly around for what seemed like forever. Reluctantly, she agreed and allowed Foote to guide her through the crowd to a friendly-looking seafood restaurant that had quaint tables on a wrought-iron balcony overlooking Bourbon Street.

They picked out a table upstairs on the balcony and ordered their food (Foote had offered an endearing, quizzical enquiry as to why Claire had ordered the shrimp jambalaya *'in her condition'*—she found his concern to be quite refreshingly touching) and a matching duo of beers. On the street below them, an impromptu jazz procession happened by, the music loud, raucous and so incredibly full of life. Claire watched, rapt as the procession snaked by until the last of the musicians and drunkenly dancing followers had disappeared down St. Louis, and for the first time since arriving in the city, she had the faint semblance of a smile on her lips.

The band were playing a Louis Armstrong number—a jazzed-up version of *Wonderful World,* and as they vanished down St. Louis Street, a random pair of synapses fired simultaneously deep in Claire's brain and triggered a startlingly lucid memory.

"That's it," she said.

"What's what?" Foote countered, as he peered down on to the street.

"I remember St. Louis," she told him. "I remember him walking me down there a ways, and there's an art gallery and a voodoo shop—a proper one, not one filled with all that tourist crap. The club was through that." She tapped furiously at her cell phone screen for confirmation. "Papa Doc's."

"After the Cambodian guy?" Foote ventured.

"Haitian, but yes, that's the one alright."

"You're sure that's the one?"

"As sure as I can be, Ethan." Claire didn't dare doubt herself. She knew that time was against them, could feel Richard's presence, as if he were there in the city with them and was standing at her shoulder. She and Foote had already spent far too long traipsing the length and breadth of Bourbon Street and its tributaries, and all she had to go on were a handful of fuzzy memories of a drunken night twelve months ago. If this hunch wasn't right, it was safe to say that they were pretty much screwed.

***

Of course, Claire's gut feeling about her husband had been correct. Richard had finally made it to New Orleans and was feeling most invigorated to be back in the city of his unholy conception; it was as if the shit-gods had preordained this from the very beginning.

He ditched the Uber car on the outskirts and opted to walk the rest of the way, it was a wonderful evening, and it wasn't as if he didn't already know where his wife would be heading—even if she didn't know yet.

***

Detective Howgard swung her car into the parking garage and found a spot-on level three, one above where Claire had parked up; the GPS had lost the signal at the entryway to the garage, but you really didn't need to be Sherlock Holmes to figure out where Jepson-Richard's crappy vehicle would be.

She got out and walked down the concrete ramp to check out the Camry, the muscles in her legs complaining angrily with each step, and her head throbbing like a crazy thing. The car offered up no clues; its engine was cold, and two of the tires were badly in need of replacing, but that was all. It would be down to good old police work and a healthy smattering of good luck from hereon in.

Howgard knew all too well that she was putting both

her career and her reputation on the line with this one. She was way out of her jurisdiction, and the paperwork would be horrendous when this was all over, not to mention the potential fallout if she failed. But, this wouldn't be the first time the detective had followed a hunch and hit pay dirt. The last time, they'd even given her a fucking medal.

Only problem now was why had Claire Jepson-Richards come all this way to New Orleans, and where the fuck would she go?

FIFTEEN

Claire had wolfed down her dinner, despite her desperate urge to flee the restaurant and get herself to the seedy club she knew in her gut skulked somewhere along St. Louis Street. Foote had almost had to physically restrain her as she grew increasingly impatient for their food to arrive, advising her as diplomatically as he could that she needed some sustenance inside her - even if only for the baby's sake—before embarking on the final part of their surreal quest. Claire had considered protesting and storming away from the petite wooden table, with its red gingham tablecloth and decorative condiment set, when her usually sedate baby had begun kicking up a storm in her womb. It was as if the thing was picking up on its mother's tension and was trying to punch its way out through her abdomen.

The jambalaya was delicious and gave Claire chronic heartburn, as she gulped it down in huge forkfuls, like it had been her first meal in days. Foote followed suit with his own meal. He, too, was hungry and eager to be done with the unsavory business they had in the city.

...and Then You Die

Claire paid the bill with a credit card Richard had stolen from Rachel's pocket the night before and was almost surprised that the transaction went through without a hitch; obviously the deliciously daring Rachel and Roberto hadn't been missed too much just yet.

After what had seemed an unbearable age, but had actually only been forty minutes or so, Claire led Foote out of the restaurant, and once again, they were back into the busy hubbub of Bourbon Street. She tugged on his hand to pull him against the tide of revelers, taking the lead herself this time. Just before they reached the corner of St. Louis, Claire spotted a pharmacy and pulled her companion inside. In the bright, overly air-conditioned store, Claire made a beeline to the aisle over which hung a large sign that declared: *heartburn/stomach*. She grabbed a bottle of heartburn tablets to counteract the gnawing acidity that assaulted the back of her throat and then proceeded to fill her basket with a pile of blue boxes that jostled and rattled as she made her way to the register.

The girl on the register looked to be little more than a teenager. She wore her greasy, mouse-brown hair scraped back in a tight ponytail that was tied up with what looked like a rubber band and made the spotty skin on her face appear taut. She counted through the boxes in the pregnant lady's basket and rung up each and every one of them, whilst casting a wary eye over Claire and the man mountain with whom she stood hip to hip. No doubt, the cashier girl thought to herself, they were making some new kind of street drug with this stuff, although exactly what high one could expect to get from the stuff was beyond her. She smiled sweetly at the odd-looking couple, her mouthful of steel braces glinting in the stark fluorescent light, and she decided to say nothing.

Claire paid the girl—the unfortunate Rachel's card again—and bustled from the store, clutching the bulging plastic carrier bag that was emblazoned with a generic *'thank you for your custom'*. She paused on the corner of Bourbon and St. Louis to catch her breath and attempt to bring under control all the thoughts that were bouncing around inside her head, like kittens in a tumble dryer.

"You okay, Miss Jepson?" Foote smiled down at her. "You don't have to do this, you know; there must be another way-"

Claire silenced him with a finger to his lips. "There is no other way, Ethan. And, yes, yes, I do have to do this. You are the one who has a choice here."

"You mean…?" A look of hurt settled on the man's giant face.

"You got me this far, and I'll always be grateful for that." Claire clutched his hand with her free one. "But this isn't your fight."

"I'm not leaving you to face this—*that*—alone, Miss Jepson. I've come this far, and I'll be damned if I'm gonna bail on you now."

"Thank you, Ethan." Claire hugged him. Her arms were unable to reach all the way around his expansive chest, and she could hear his heart beating.

The voodoo store was exactly where Claire's jogged memory had remembered it to be. In fact, it looked exactly the same as it had in her mind's eye—the owners were clearly not as fastidious in changing their window display as perhaps they should have been. The door stood open, casting Papa Doc's light and cool, incense infused air out into the quiet street; very few Bourbon Street revelers ventured this far from the bright lights, strip joints, and deafening jazz music.

As was typical of the voodoo stores in New Orleans,

Papa Doc's was crammed ceiling to floor with all manner of *magik* paraphernalia, amulets, tarot, artifacts, and hundreds upon hundreds of books. There were fake skulls—animal and human—voodoo dolls, mysterious sounding herbs in little gauze bags, animal body parts—dried and pickled—and a vast array of bleached bones, and good luck charms. Towards the rear of the store, the smell changed to something a little more herb-like, and the animal parts and supposed human bones somehow appeared more real.

Claire and Foote followed a small group of people into the store. Two of the group—a couple of hipster gay guys—browsed the clutter of voodoo and hoodoo merchandise whilst the three girls in their group made their way purposefully towards the back of the store, where they disappeared behind a dusty, diaphanous curtain.

"Can I help ya?" a voice from behind the counter enquired as Claire and Foote walked in.

"Just looking, thank you." Claire smiled.

"Looking for anything in particular?" The owner of the voice popped up from behind the cash register.

Something in the tone of the voice made Claire turn around, and she was faced with a skinny, strangely androgynous person who stood tall behind the glass counter. The person—Claire genuinely had no idea as to what sex it was meant to be—had a thin, pinched face with a wan complexion that appeared damp and waxy. It smiled at Claire, thin lips parting to reveal an uneven set of yellowed teeth, and Claire considered it a knowing smile.

"I was here before," Claire ventured. "There was a club," she played her hunch.

"Still is," the peculiar creature said, its voice deadpan. Its eyes flicked towards the curtain that hung at the back of the store then back to Claire.

"And?" Foote shuffled forwards, his thighs pressing against the counter.

"And if you've been here before, then you'll know what to expect," the guy/gal let its contempt slip out.

"How much to get in?"

"Are you sure you've been here before?"

Claire rubbed her belly, as much to quieten her fidgeting offspring as to emphasize her condition. "Quite sure," she said.

"It's free for the right people, two drink minimum, though," the assistant told her. "Are you sure you want to go in with *that*?"

At first Claire assumed the assistant was referring to her pregnancy. Then she saw that (*he, she, it?*) was staring intently at Foote, like he was something to be scraped from the bottom of a shoe.

"Quite sure," Claire tried not to sound too offended on her friend's behalf.

The assistant nodded towards the curtain and sat back down on the wooden chair it had secreted behind the counter. The chair creaked loudly as if its occupant was somehow too heavy for it, as if it were mocking the assistant's slight, shifting stature.

Claire waddled to the rear of the store; Foote close behind her. She brushed by the gay couple, who gave her a steely gaze and *tut-tutted* their offence at her lack of manners, irrespective of how ungainly and pregnant she was.

Behind the curtain—which smelled of incense, weed and something altogether more corporeal—lay a wide metal door set in a steel frame. The door was a tarnished silvery-gray color, pitted with myriad dents and scratches; it looked like there had been a hell of a lot of people over the years who had been desperate to claw their way into the delights that lay beyond.

"Are we supposed to knock?" Foote asked, as he searched the sheet of metal for a handle. Found nothing.

"I guess so." Claire rapped her knuckles on the cold steel, and almost immediately, the door swung silently open.

***

More than anything, it was the unearthly stink that made the biggest and most lasting first impression of the secret club that spread out behind the steel door. Above the foul odor of excrement, the air was crammed with the ammonia stench of stale urine, vomit, and all the unclean smells of the fluids of sex blended less than subtly with the sharp tang of the sweat of exertion and pain.

Claire remembered the club's unique reek, and it conjured vivid memories that careened through her brain in an endless stream—it's true that smell is the strongest invoker of memories amongst all the senses—and she recalled clearly the first time she'd experienced the club, with its pounding music and heaving, sweating bodies. She even recognized one of the bartenders—he of the rock-hard abs and deliciously salted perspiration. He was reclining on the bar whilst a gaggle of giddy, semi-naked girls sucked tequila from his navel.

Claire and Foote made their way passed the incredibly attractive doorwoman, who was naked save for silver nipple rings and a miniscule triangle of leather that had been stapled to her vulva. She smiled as Claire and Foote walked by and absently wiped her fingers in the thin trickle of blood that made its way down along her thigh.

The club was heaving; the dance floor sticky with excrement and puddles of piss that made it quite treacherous for walking, especially for someone like Claire who could barely see their own feet. A solid mass of semi-clad and naked people danced with abandon to the tuneless rhythm that thudded through the room, arms flailing, feet slipping, oblivious to everything around them.

Claire forced her way through the crowd, pushing the carousers out of her way with elbows, shoulders and belly. She was single-minded in her determination to get to a place at the rear of the club that she remembered all too well.

There were no dancers there. The bare concrete walls and floor were instead littered with people in all manner of lewd, depraved acts. This was the playroom.

Claire stepped around the writhing, naked bodies with a purpose—she was searching for that particular *something,* whose memory lurked in the darkest shadows at the farthest corner of her brain, as if it were too timid to venture out into the open. It tormented Claire like an itch she just couldn't scratch, and she knew—*just knew*—that whatever it was, it held the answer to why she had sought out this disgusting place.

At Claire's feet were two old-ish, doughy men who were both completely naked and smeared in what looked like clotted blood. They were holding up a young woman's legs, so her back was on the hard floor and her ass—help agape by a stainless-steel speculum—was vertical. A trio of women—older, by far, than their receptacle—were taking turns to hawk and spit into the stretched circular hole that the girl's asshole presented. Claire could see that the dark hole was almost full to the brim with slimy, green-streaked saliva and knew that soon enough the men would remove the speculum and have the girl shit out the contents of her rectum into their eager mouths.

"It has to be here somewhere," Claire grumbled.

"What are we looking for exactly?" Foote asked.

"I don't know." Claire sounded exasperated. "But I'll know it when I see-" She blundered headlong into a pair of giggling, young girls who were laid out on the floor in a glistening, shit-streaked sixty-nine and were taking it in turns to fart loudly into each other's mouths. "I am so sorry," Claire blustered, her face flushed with embarrassment. "I didn't see you there." She patted her belly for emphasis; most things adjacent to her feet had become invisible in the past month or so.

"That's okay." The girl on top smiled. "Why don't you join us?" She poked a playful finger into her companion's puckered anus, and the girl giggled and squirmed.

"Thank you, no," Claire declined politely, as alluring as the lithe young girls looked, she'd had enough of ass-play to last her a lifetime. "I'm looking for something…"

"More?"

Claire spun around to greet the voice that had piped up behind her from out of the blue.

It belonged to an elderly man of slight build and wizened features, who looked like he belonged in a *Harry Potter* movie. In keeping with the majority of those playing their filthy games around Claire and Foote, the old guy was naked save for a tiny rubber apron that failed to hide his long, thin, dangling dick. In one hand he held a zinc bucket, which slopped perilously full with a brown/gray liquid that looked—and smelled—like something that had been forcibly coaxed from the anal glands of a hideous sea creature. Atop the foul liquid floated a fat, lumpy turd and several chunks of what looked to be regurgitated fish heads.

The man crouched down next to the farting girls and thrust his hand between the legs of the girl on top. She moaned and raised her hips, and his hand came away slick. Carefully, he scraped the thin film of the young girl's pussy juice from his hand on the rim of the bucket. The thick mucus slid the short distance into the congealing mess in the bucket, and the old man looked pleased with himself.

"Something like that." Claire felt like she was about to throw up—she'd spotted a used, bloated tampon bobbing about in the bucket—but figured that her hurling would only serve to further delight the old boy.

"Woman in your condition might like some of that." The old man pointed to a young couple off to his right. The girl was holding her guy's head down in a bucket filled with liquid shit. She pulled him up by the hair so he could gasp a breath of fetid air then she plunged him down again. As Claire watched, the man's head remained submerged, and his arms began to flail, but still, his woman wouldn't relinquish her grip.

"I was here before, last year," Claire explained to the old man. "There was another place, here, but not here, and I need to find it." She took a deep breath, gagged at the stink that flooded her lungs. "I'm in trouble, you have to help me."

"Any trouble you got yourself into, missy, you brought it on yourself. Folk don't come here without knowing what they want."

"The lady asked for your help." Foote loomed over the old man, his shadow swallowing his skinny frame up.

"I was brought here against my will," Claire was trying her level best not to sound like a feeble, desperate victim. "It's not fair. For all I know, I was fucking *roofied*!"

"Ah," said the old man, and Claire thought she could see just the faintest hint of fear in his yellowed old eyes as he squinted up at Foote. "So that was *you*." And with that, he scurried away, his bucket of sickening slop splashing out over anyone who got in his way.

"Follow him." Claire gave Foote a shove in the back; he'd become mesmerized by two grotesquely fat men who were busy writing on an equally corpulent woman's pendulous breasts with their own shit, which had created a thick, smudged font on her pasty skin. One guy had written *WHORE*, the other, *SLUT,* and they stood back to admire their handiwork as the woman stood spread-eagled before them with an odd, benign smile on her face. Upon closer inspection, it became clear that the fat woman had been nailed to the wall by rusted metal spikes through her hands and feet.

Claire's push broke the spell, and Foote set off after the wrinkled old man, doing his best not to tread on the slippery, naked people under foot or slip on the excrement and juices that their debauched cavorting created.

Claire followed on, slipstreaming behind Foote to avoid the worst of the throng of hedonists, most of who seemed to be inexplicably attracted to her bloated, pregnant body. On more than one occasion, she had cause to slap away hands that groped most impolitely at her distended stomach and milk-filled tits.

The old man disappeared; the last Claire saw of him was his scrawny old backside, that reminded her of a raisin, vanishing into the dark shadows way over in the far corner of the club. There were no people at all that far back, as if the darkness there was holding sentry over something forbidden and deeply unpleasant.

Claire dared herself to venture onwards, stepping around the last of the playing people—an elderly woman with her foot buried up to the ankle in a young, muscular guy's split ass—she made her way into the shadows, one hand gripping Foote's. In her other, she held on tightly to her plastic carrier bag, like her life depended upon it.

There was a sharp turn at the corner of the room, from which led a narrow hallway. The hallway itself was pitch black and punctuated by a sporadic line of tiny yellow lights that were swallowed by the gloom. Claire turned the corner, and immediately, the raucous noise of the club diminished, as if the shadows were somehow dampening it. The club's ungodly stench didn't diminish in the slightest. If anything, it seemed to be getting stronger.

"You can't be down here," a strong, overly masculine voice boomed through the gloom. "Go back to the club."

Claire strained her eyes and made out the vague shape of someone—something—huge a little further down the hallway. "I'm looking for..." Claire faltered, none too sure about exactly what she was looking for. All she knew was that this dark, claustrophobic passage felt somehow *right*.

"You won't find what you're looking for down here," the voice growled, menacing. "Whatever that is, so I suggest that you fuck off."

Foote pushed by Claire in the dark. His brusque action pinned her to the warm wall and made her baby kick out in annoyance.

Foote felt his way along towards the shape that skulked at the end of the hallway. As his eyes quickly grew accustomed to the darkness, he could make out a naked black guy of about his own size.

"I thought I told you to fuck off," the big guy menaced, as Foote stood toe to toe with him.

"What's down there?" Foot ignored the man's rudeness. He could see that there was orange, flickering light glowing from a narrow archway behind the guy, and it piqued his interest more than could be put off by some meathead doorman.

Behind the sentry, the thin gap in the smooth wall opened out onto an elaborately cast, iron spiral staircase, which plunged downwards into the flickering gloom below. The struts of the staircase were fashioned in the shape of contorted, broken-limbed people with gaping, screaming mouths and tormented faces, and the steps themselves denoted thick, bulging penises that were plunged deep into wrought-iron ripped anuses.

"Nothing that concerns you," the big shape replied, and it dawned on Foote that he couldn't actually make out the guy's face.

Claire's attack of *deja vu* hit her like a punch to the gut and physically knocked the breath from her. "This is it," she gasped. "You have to let us through."

"I don't have to do anything, miss," the voice boomed with a hint of an accent now—sounded like something fake German from the old war movies.

Ethan hit the man. Hard. He lashed out with the heel of his hand at where instinct told him the man's nose would be, and he felt the satisfying crunch as he found his mark. The man's unseen nose exploded its cartilage and thin slivers of bone into his brain, and he slumped forward into Foote's arms.

"You killed him?" Claire was suitably horrified.

"Looks like, Miss Jepson," Foote replied without emotion. "We can go through now." Foote lowered the deceased doorman gently to the floor; the front of his shirt was soaked through with the man's blood and snot.

"Thank you, Ethan," Claire's voice trembled as she rested a hand on her friend's arm, felt his tendons tense beneath the tanned skin. And for the first time, she was truly afraid of him.

***

Whilst Claire and Ethan were navigating their way through the sights and disgusting smells of the scat club, Detective Howgard was waiting to be served at the pharmacy and listening in on the conversation the young assistant in the white laboratory coat was having with her particularly unattractive, pizza-faced colleague.

"I don't know what she was thinking, buying that many, especially with her being so pregnant an' all, but ya don't like to say anything, do ya?" the girl said. "Totally cleaned us out. Now I'm gonna have to remind Mr. Hopkins to put another order in."

"Ya should have refused to serve her," Pizza-face advised, as he absently picked at a grotesque pustule that sprouted from his neck; it looked to Howgard like he was budding a second head.

"Nah, she could have been high on something nasty and ended up eating my face." The girl grimaced. "And did you see the size of that guy she was with? No *way* was I going to say anything."

The girl's colleague nodded sagely and mumbled something beneath his breath that Howgard didn't quite catch.

Howgard couldn't believe her ears. It just *had* to be Jepson-Richards they were talking about, and it sounded like she had hooked up with her security guard, too! Howgard loved being proved right – she had just known those two were in cahoots! In the end though, it had just come down to dumb luck. Howgard had popped into the pharmacy for something to ease the headache that had grown behind her eyes as she'd trawled Bourbon Street and its questionable delights. Dumb luck rather than good police work, wasn't that always the way? Still, she consoled herself, it was good police work that had gotten her this far, didn't she deserve just a little luck?

"Next," the white-coated girl couldn't have sounded more disinterested in her job if she'd tried.

Howgard slammed the white bottle of generic Ibuprofen on the countertop, and the girl looked startled. "The couple you were just talking about," she gave her best shot at an amiable smile, "which way did they go?"

"That way, down St. Louis," the girl said, as she rung up Howgard's purchase. "Said something about 'Doc's shop. That'll be three dollars sixty-nine." She held out her hand for payment and seemed most surprised when the cop gave her cash. It was almost as if she'd never seen a five-dollar bill before.

"Thank you." Howgard smiled and rushed from the store without waiting for her change.

She arrived at Papa Doc's a little out of breath having half-walked, half-ran most of the length of St. Louis. She'd paused only to swallow some of the drugs she'd just bought, having realized, to her chagrin, that in her haste, she'd forgotten to buy water. So, Howgard had crunched the foul things down dry, and they'd left a hellish aftertaste in her mouth.

Howgard stumbled into the voodoo store and flashed her badge at the doped-up guy (girl?), who sat behind the counter and hoped that he/she didn't spot that the shield was from out of state. "A heavily pregnant woman and a large guy?" she panted.

Still more dumb luck: the assistant barely even glanced at the detective's badge and nodded nonchalantly towards the back of the store, where Howgard saw a shabby curtain that hung adjacent to a statue of Baphomet wearing a baseball cap, upon which was embroidered '*I love N.O*'.

"Thanks," Howgard said as the assistant returned

its attention to the book on its lap. Howgard made her way to the back of the store, her nose wrinkling at the pungent odor that hung thick in the air.

***

The spiral staircase descended deep into the sewers that ran beneath the club. This Claire thought to be inevitable, all things considered. She made her way down towards the flickering glow with slow, deliberate steps; she'd slipped off her shoes to avoid making a sound on the stairs, and the metal felt cool and damp against her bare feet.

"Stinks like the sewers," Foote whispered the obvious from behind Claire. He'd pulled his shirt collar up over his nose against the putrid stench, and his voice was muffled. "What are these people, ninja turtles?"

Claire stifled a giggle and continued on; the circle of the staircase was beginning to make her more than a little dizzy.

Voices.

The inimitable sounds of someone in great and agonizing pain.

Coming from somewhere deep within the candle lit gloom, the noises resonated loudly and echoed up from the tunnels like piped music in a dark elevator.

A woman's scream pierced the darkness. It was shrill and pleading, and it made Claire hesitate a little and wonder if this really was the best idea after all. Inside her womb, her child turned a somersault and kicked out at her kidneys—as if in its own reply to the self-doubt.

After what seemed an age of walking in circles, Claire and Foote reached the bottom of the staircase and stepped out into a round tunnel that was only just tall enough to accommodate her height. Foote, unfortunately, had to stoop his head forward in an ungainly Quasimodo posture in order to walk. At their feet scurried myriad rats, some the size of small dogs, but fortunately, the critters were far more frightened of the intruders than vice versa. The rounded walls were damp and oozed water, and were populated by a living coat of shimmering cockroaches. The vile insects twitched and jostled, as Claire and Foote shuffled by, and they waved their antennae towards the humans to catch a taste of them.

Coating the floor of the tunnel was a thin layer of slimy mud—only it wasn't mud, Claire knew that much—which squished slick and cool between Claire's bare toes. In actual fact, the stuff really didn't bother her all that much; she'd experienced far worse during her time with Richard, the Shit Monster. As she and Foote walked on towards the eerie glow and the breathy screams, the rats went about their business around their feet, and unseen things crawled and scuttled over the glistening walls and above their heads.

The glow of a thousand candles greeted Claire's light-starved eyes as she neared the end of the tunnel, and the guttural screams resounded sporadically and sent chilled fingers down Claire's spine.

"Wow," Foote whispered as they reached their destination. "What the fuck is this place?"

Claire looked over her shoulder at her companion's awestruck face that was bathed in warm yellow light, and found that she was lost for words.

Before them lay a great chamber. It was a cavernous atrium built of the same shiny red brick as the sewer tunnels that punctuated its circumference; it looked to all intents and purposes as if the place had been purposefully built back in the eighteen-thirties as an integral part of the sewer system. Although, what possible purpose it served as within the waste disposal system was unclear. That left only one conclusion in Claire's mind; the place was built for a whole different purpose entirely, most likely to do with the weird cults she had read about.

"They've been doing this forever," she whispered to herself.

Claire craned her neck to look up at the ceiling of the atrium, but it was hidden by a murky darkness even the multitude of fat candles couldn't dispel. All she could see were the dozens of towering arches of brick that reached high up above her to support it.

Keeping her body pressed up against the clammy brick wall despite the scuttling insects, Claire ventured a little father forward. She was eager to see the source of the voices and desperate to know what was going on down there. She mentally crossed her fingers and toes and hoped against hope that here she would find what she was looking for.

In the dead center of the expansive chamber, Claire could make out what appeared to be some kind of well. It stood only a couple of bricks high and was filled to overflowing with the rippling, gurgling mess of what could only have been human waste. A stride or three away from the well stood an altar that looked as if it had been carved out of solid excreta. Its sides were decorated with the most elaborate and ornate carvings that depicted acts of defecation and coprophagia by people, a variety of animals, half-people and fecal spirits all entwined together in what looked to be one almighty shit orgy.

Upon the altar lay a naked and incredibly pregnant lady. Her fecund belly bulged upwards towards the dark, enshrouded ceiling and was heaving as she screamed out her birthing pains. She was held fast to the alter by a quartet of muscular, naked men - one gripping each of her struggling, sweat greased limbs—who were entirely devoid of hair and streaked with the unmistakable stains of feces, which appeared to form strange symbols and letterings.

By the woman's head, there stood a tall man who fidgeted and shuffled and looked for all the world like the nervous, expectant father—stick a fat, fuck-off cigar in his mouth, Claire mused, and the illusion would have been complete. He, too, was completely naked, and his form appeared soft, squishy, and fuzzy around the edges, in the manner in which Richard was prone when he'd gone too long without feeding. If Claire had remembered her research correctly, this ostensibly concerned father-to-be was the woman's fecal spirit.

Claire gagged on the stream of barely digested Cajun food that spurted up to the back of her throat, as the realization hit her that what she was witnessing was her own fate, and that thought terrified her.

As if sensing her anxiety, Foote draped a heavy arm around Claire's shoulders and drew her body in tight against his.

A big part of Claire—the abject coward who hated confrontation—wanted nothing more than to run away from the grim scene, even if that did mean a lifetime of hiding from Richard. But there was still a small part of her that knew that she had to face up to her fears and put an end to the nightmare she'd been living ever since the stranger had seduced her. And there was an even smaller part of Claire Jepson who wanted to race up to that hellish altar and save the poor woman and the child, which was doomed even before it drew its first breath.

It was as she contemplated that particular course of action that Claire saw a white-robed figure approaching the altar. The figure had the unmistakable stature and gait of a man of true importance—clearly a high priest of some impressive magnitude—his head and face were completely covered by the robe's heavy hood. As he strode with sinister purpose towards the altar, the man's impossibly white, pristine robe billowed out behind him, like some earth-bound cloud, and gave him an almost ghost-like air. Surrounding the robed man were a dozen naked acolytes—a half dozen of each sex—who kept up a steady pace behind him. Once he arrived at the foot of the altar, they all fanned out and took up equidistant positions around the perimeter of the room.

"And so it is," the man unfastened his robe, "that we summon this fresh life in order that our brethren may walk for eternity amongst the mortals." He pulled the robe away from his supple, tanned body and let it fall to the ground.

"It's him," Claire mumbled, andfor a split second, she thought she may have said it too loud and given their presence away. Luckily, the incomprehensible, tuneless reply that was chanted by the nude onlookers drowned out her voice. Claire clamped a hand over her mouth and stared wide-eyed at the man she'd last seen through a drunken haze, as he sodomized her in a luxury hotel suite.

The High Priest positioned himself between the splayed legs of the gravid woman upon the altar and maneuvered his not inconsiderable penis into her gaping cunt. The man-thing by the woman's head looked on passively, his own dick limp and lifeless.

The woman screamed to high heaven, and her voice soared up into the vaulted ceiling, where it was swallowed eagerly by the inky shadows.

Claire watched with a sick fascination as the High Priest—her own seducer—thrust his cock deep into the writhing woman. The woman cried out her agonies as her body pushed out with the spasms of parturition and against the dick that swelled inside her. All the while, Claire worked feverishly at the bubble packets in her carrier bag, painfully aware of every *click*, *pop* and *rustle* her activities were creating.

A gush of steaming fluids cascaded from the altar woman's groin. It soaked the High Priest's dangling ball sack and the entirety of his powerful legs. The taut mound of the woman's belly gave a sickening lurch, and she screamed blue murder and struggled against the strong hands that held her.

The High Priest pulled out, his giant prick slick with juice and blood; it bobbed about, like some exotic fishing lure, and actually looked *disappointed*. The priest reached between the woman's legs with both hands and grasped at the slippery, bluish-pink thing that bulged out of her straining vagina.

"Oh, sweet Jesus, no," Claire muttered, as she saw the baby crowning. "We can't let them..." She felt Foote's arm tighten about her shoulders, and an unspoken reassurance passed between them both.

There was a sickeningly audible noise of rending flesh as the woman's vagina split, and her child's head burst out from her body. She yowled through the pain as blood and slop poured from her, and her womb gave one final heave, and the woman slumped against the cold, moist altar, spent. The High Priest grasped the baby's head and pulled it gently out from its mother's body. With the head free and the vagina torn, the remainder of the child slipped out like an over ripe banana from its blackening peel.

The fecal spirit, who throughout had remained standing by the mother's lolling head, shuffled towards the business end of the altar, the stout nubs of its tendrils taking shape in eager anticipation along the entirety of his abhorrent frame. Quickly, they grew and reached out blindly towards the mewling infant, homing in on its cries.

The High Priest lifted the child to his mouth and chomped down on the twisted, rubbery umbilical cord, and a cascade of dark blood poured down his chin to paint his broad, muscular chest crimson red. Thus, disconnected from its mother, the baby was duly offered to the approaching fecal spirit.

Seizing her chance—her only chance—Claire dashed out from her hiding place. Foote followed close behind, his heavy steps echoing loudly around the humid chamber. "Stop it!" Claire screamed so loud that she tasted blood in her throat.

"Who dares interrupt?" The High Priest bellowed, as he saw Claire sprinting towards him—was that a hint of recognition in his eyes?

Claire hurled a fistful of green tablets at the fecal spirit, as the first of its brown, oozing tendrils caressed the baby's bloodied body. Behind her, a pair of the naked celebrants made a move towards her with violence written in their faces. They were batted away by Foote like they were just troublesome flies.

The tablets eagerly found their mark and stuck to the fecal spirit's pliant flesh where they were quickly absorbed into the shifting skin. The spirit recoiled, as if he had been struck by acid, and the gruesome tendrils retracted with such force that the thing staggered backwards and almost lost his footing.

"*Loperamide!*" the spirit squealed at the top of his voice, and almost immediately, his body began to stiffen, and the moist sheen on his skin visibly evaporated.

"How dare you!" the High Priest admonished Claire. Angry beyond comprehension, he held the baby out in front of his chest, as if it were a shield, but noticeably, he stayed put, his wary eyes not straying from what Claire held in her hand.

The fecal spirit, and would-be surrogate father of the newborn, dropped to his knees and clutched at his throat. His mouth flapped open and closed with silent screams, yet only a fine, beige dust puffed from his cracked lips. As he collapsed, clumps of desiccated flesh crumbled from his body to reveal the dull bones and shriveled organs beneath.

Claire watched, with morbid fascination, as the fecal spirit rapidly came undone and disintegrated before her eyes. Behind her, the naked acolytes broke circle to advance on both her and Foote, their pasty flesh rippling and wobbling in the dancing candlelight.

The High Priest held up a hand to still his congregation, his eyes fearful and still trained on the contents of the intruder's right hand.

As the fecal spirit collapsed without further ceremony into little more than a smear of powdery dust on the dank sewer floor, Claire rounded on the High Priest.

"Put. The. Baby. Down. Motherfucker," she growled, all the while fighting the overwhelming feeling of nausea that was brought about by the stench of spilled blood, the piscine aroma of birthing fluids, and the all-pervading sewer stench. Claire raised her clenched hand to her shoulder and made an almost imperceptible throwing motion. She smiled as the High Priest flinched. Claire's belly churned as her own baby stirred within her, a show of solidarity for the newborn that keened loudly in the priest's grasp.

The priest stepped back towards the altar. His bare feet slipped on the blood and slime, and he was forced to steady himself against the altar with his thighs. In what was an almost tender gesture, he lay the baby gently down on its mother's chest, and Claire saw, for the first time, that the infant was a boy; its balls huge, swollen and grotesquely pink and vein-blue between its chubby, curled legs.

The baby's mother stirred a little in response, and she draped a weak, weary arm over her child and drew it to her breast. There it settled against her warm, damp skin and suckled voraciously at her distended teat.

"Get them!" The High Priest shrieked at the top of his voice, and he sounded more like a hysterical old woman than the epitome of masculinity that his human form presented.

The nude followers ran towards Claire and Foote, their sudden burst of jiggling movement providing just the distraction the priest needed to make a run for it. He darted away from the altar, away from Claire's aim with those dreaded tablets, and off towards the welcoming sanctuary of the shadows at the far side of the atrium.

Half of the acolytes crashed into Foote, their combined weight still not enough to topple him. He lashed out with his hard, meaty fists and broke two noses and pulverized a jaw into quivering Jello before the acolytes even knew what was happening. Another four piled into the melee and clambered up Foote's huge frame as one would scale a challenging mountain peak. Foote flailed and grabbed at the slick bodies, his strong fingers dug hard into doughy breasts, popped vulnerable testes, and dislocated the dangling cocks that slapped impotently against him. Yet still they came at him, their onslaught relentless, despite how hard he punched or how far he flung them. They covered Foote's body with theirs, driving him ever backwards and away from Claire.

Claire was set upon by two of the High Priest's human guard-dogs—a pert-breasted woman who looked to be barely out of her teens and a pot-bellied, bearded guy old enough to have been Claire's grandfather. Immune to Claire's threat of the green tablets—must still be human, she figured with some disdain—they rushed Claire and wrestled her to the ground. Claire panicked against the weight of naked flesh that pinned her down, and she clawed and kicked against them, oblivious to the flurry of punches that pummeled her prone body. Adding to her panic was that the handful of tablets had spilled from her hand, and the carrier bag had been knocked from her grasp.

Foote and his clinging horde of clammy flesh staggered yet farther away from Claire and only stopped when his ankle cracked hard against the lip of the well, and finally, the big man went down.

"Ethan!" Claire screamed out, as she saw how her friend was pinned beneath the seething mound of flabby, bare flesh. She could see that his assailants were busy maneuvering his vast bulk headfirst towards the stubby rim of the well. The coagulated slime confined between the crumbling bricks rippled and bubbled in anticipation.

Claire renewed her attempt to be free of her own attackers. She bucked her body and flailed her arms and legs with every ounce of strength she could muster, but all to no avail. The young girl was sitting across Claire's chest and slapped at her face with harsh, stinging swipes, with her back leaning against Claire's distended belly. For its part, Claire's fetus fought back valiantly against the girl with what felt to Claire like vicious roundhouse kicks. As Claire struggled, the girl slid closer to her head, her epilated pudendum spread plump and glistening in front of Claire's face like some overripe fruit.

The old guy sat with his entire weight on Claire's legs and bent her knees in the wrong direction, which sent jolts of pain up into her hips. Claire could feel the man's chubby fingers as they groped at her pussy through her jeans, and it made her want to throw up.

And so, between the two naked aggressors and her own cumbersome body, Claire was unable to wriggle free. And equally unable to help her friend.

They were holding Ethan's head beneath the foul pool of excrement now, and there were bubbles rising up in lazy blobs to pop with wet *splats* on its congealing surface. Ethan's muscles bulged, as his arms pushed against the clammy ground, and his legs kicked out in vain at the bodies that held him fast.

A gunshot rang out. It resonated around the brick-lined chamber like the bark of a ferocious animal.

"Freeze!" Detective Howgard yelled out her order from the mouth of the tunnel that fed into the atrium. Her over-stressed voice came out an octave higher than its norm; just what in God's name was going on down here? Between the disgusting stench and the filth-streaked nudists, her brain was having trouble just processing the bizarre tableau before her. And was that a freakin' baby?!

Taking advantage of the distraction, Claire threw her assailant from her chest with a solid thump to the left tit. She felt something inside the girl go *pop*. The young girl grabbed at her wounded breast and let out a pained grunt, as she tipped over on her side like a felled chimney stack. Claire freed up a leg and administered a sharp kick under the old guy's jaw. The man sprawled backwards with his arms windmilling and in his screaming mouth, Claire could see that he had bitten the end of his tongue clean off. Blood bubbled from his mouth as he fell, and his head made a sickening cracking noise upon connecting with the ground. The old man then laid quite still, eyes half-open, his stubby little erection wilting in the tepid air.

"Nobody move!" The cop shouted, and her voice multiplied around the cavernous brick walls until it sounded like there was a dozen of her. She walked towards the scattered group of people, not entirely sure where she should be pointing her gun. The woman on the altar appeared to be alive at the very least, so the cop decided upon the larger of the groups—*why were all these people naked in the sewer?* Howgard could see that she was too late to save the big guy the weirdos had been merrily drowning in what looked to be a well filled with diarrhea; his body lay inert and spattered with the stinking brown goo. His head was still submerged, its slick dome bobbing ever so slightly up and down.

Claire espied a movement in the farthest reaches of the sewer, a flash of pallid skin amongst the inky shadows and red brick arches. The High Priest was still here, searching for a way out that didn't involve a trigger-happy detective.

She still had a chance.

Claire scooted towards the altar, putting it between herself and the detective's line of sight. She snatched up the carrier bag that lay adjacent to the lifeless old man and dragged it along with her. The bag snagged on the man's ragged, yellow toenails, and half of its contents spilled out. Claire cursed beneath her breath.

Howgard now stood in the middle of the naked people. They had all taken to sitting on the cold brick sewer floor with their hands behind their heads and fingers knitted together in surrender. Not one of them looked at the detective, nor uttered a sound. She figured she really ought to retrieve the dead guy from the well but couldn't bring herself to touch his shit-soaked body. *Leave that one for forensics*, she thought. Somewhere in the background she heard a crackling sound that reminded her of the toasted rice cereal she loved as a kid.

With a fresh fistful of green tablets, Claire darted

out from her hiding place as fast as her waddling bulk would allow, with her feet skidding in a most ungainly fashion on the ground.

"I said *don't move!*" Howgard shouted towards the sudden movement. But by the time she'd swung her gun around, Claire was concealed betwixt the brick arches. The detective made her way over to the altar.

Claire ducked and darted and used the arches for cover. So intent on securing his escape was the High Priest that Claire was upon him before he knew what was happening. She grabbed him from behind and coiled an arm around his throat. "Move and I'll ram these down your fucking throat," she growled in his ear. She raised her fist up to eye level and showed him its contents so that he'd know she meant business.

"Imodium?" Howgard chuntered to herself, as she prodded with the toe of her boot at the empty drug packets that lay scattered on the floor. "What the fuck?" She glanced up at the woman who lay nursing her infant on the flaking altar. She was bleeding quite heavily from her vagina and appeared to be in bad shape; Howgard figured it was time to call in back up.

"Don't shoot!" Claire called out, as she emerged from the shadows. She coaxed the High Priest along with gentle pushes of her belly in his back, and he shuffled out from the concealment of the arches with the full strength of Claire's arm constricting his throat. As he walked, his eyes bulged ever so slightly, and his formidable dick slapped from leg to leg.

"Let him go." Howgard pointed her gun at Claire; not at all confident she could fire without taking at least part of the naked guy's head off. "We can all walk out of here, Claire."

"You have to let me do this, Detective." Claire fought to keep her voice steady and in control. "I promise I will explain this to you when we're done."

"You can explain to me when you've let him go, Claire," the detective insisted. "Whatever he's done, it's not worth getting yourself killed over." Howgard squinted through the gloom as Claire and her captive continued their steady walk towards the center of the room. What was she threatening the guy with? Diarrhea tablets?!

"They're going to kill my baby." Emotion laced Claire's voice. "Then they'll kill me. And you too."

"Nobody's going to harm your baby, Claire," Howgard told her. "I promise."

"You can't promise that, Detective. They almost got her baby, and now they want mine." Claire nodded towards the altar, then back to the guy under her control. "And he's the only one who can prevent it from happening." She sounded as if she was about to cry.

A dozen things flew around in Howgard's mind like fluttering bats that were impossible to catch. Had she stumbled upon some sick, satanic baby-killing cult? What if the obviously insane Jepson lady was actually telling the truth? What the fuck was a detective supposed to do now? Should she let this play out and put more lives at risk?

Claire and the High Priest reached the altar, fewer than three strides away from the detective, four at the most.

Against her better judgment, Howgard lowered her gun.

"Please, don't let her-" The High Priest sniveled.

"Shut the fuck up," Claire snarled and pushed the man forwards with a rough shove. His thighs slammed against the altar, and he doubled over with a loud grunt across the legs of the nursing mother. She yelped and kicked him away, and a fresh spurt of blood spurted out from between her legs. The priest stood up and turned to face Claire, his eyes still glued to the green tablets in her hand.

"What do you want from me?" he asked.

"I want you to revoke the thing that I married," Claire growled, "before he kills me and my baby."

"I…I can't…"

"You can, and you fucking will!" Claire raised her voice and hand, and the High Priest winced. "You are the only one who *can* do it—since you made him."

"With you," the priest offered up a wry smile. "You were delightfully willing, as I recall."

Claire gave a wince of her own, as her baby turned somersaults inside her body. "If I'd known the shit you were getting me into, I'd have never -"

"And if I do as you ask?"

"Then I'll leave you alone to rot in whatever kind of stinking hell this is." Claire stroked her fidgeting stomach to quieten her child. "Otherwise…" She raised her throwing arm once again, and the High Priest tried to back away.

"Okay, there's no need to be hasty." The priest was sweating profusely. His entire body glistened waxy wet in the candlelight; any other location and circumstance, and he'd look spectacularly sensual. "Show yourself!" he shouted into the gloom, and his words bounced around the cavernous atrium like lost music.

"Hello, Claire," the familiar, unmistakably British accent purred from the shadows. "Thank you for coming."

SIXTEEN

Richard stepped out from the shadows with his arms spread wide, as if inviting the warmest of hugs. Behind him shuffled two young, naked women, who were presumably identical twins. One of the twins, however, appeared to be considerably *older* than the other, and she bore the telltale signs of Richard's nefarious feeding habits; her skin sagged where it should have been deliciously supple, her breasts drooped, and her body appeared deflated. Trailing from between that woman's legs was Richard's dirty, snake-like appendage that draped between his sex and hers, joining them together in a deathly link.

"How have you been, my love?" Richard smiled at his wife. "Have you missed me? Have you missed—this?" He withdrew his elongated, forked penis tendril from the twin, and it slipped from her ass and pussy with a wet smacking sound. The woman slumped back—caught by her sister—and lay propped against a brick arch with her body shaking and a thick brown glop dribbling from her vagina.

There was a commotion from across the atrium,

and Richard's attention was drawn to where the detective—momentarily distracted by his sudden arrival—had been pounced upon by the acolytes who had been passively sitting around her.

Howgard struggled against the slippery, maniacal throng that engulfed her body and scratched, punched and slapped at her. She managed to fire off a single shot before they removed the gun from her hand, but it wasn't wasted. It caught one of Howgard's assailants—a bony, lanky girl with little in the way of either breasts or ass—beneath her chin. The bullet neatly blew off the top of her skull like it was a *kippah* and sprayed her brains all across the sewer. Her legs collapsed beneath her, and she sat down heavily, the bones in her coccyx crunching loudly. She had a look of dumb bemusement on her handsome face, and the back of her head looked like it had been scooped out, like a kid's boiled egg.

"Enough!" The High Priest commanded, and his followers ceased their attack on the detective. They retained their firm hold of her, and the guy who had stolen her gun showed no intention of returning it.

Surrounded and outnumbered by such a ridiculous amount of naked and hostile flesh, Howgard had no choice but to watch, as the final act in her bizarre investigation played out and wonder just how in hell she was going to write this one up.

Richard stood in the center of the room, less than twelve feet away from Claire. She glowered at him; her fist clenched tight around the quintet of green tablets that dug into her palm.

"What are you waiting for, Claire?" The High Priest asked, his eyebrow raised quizzically.

"For you to do whatever it is you do to get this piece of crap out of my life." She pointed at Richard, who looked genuinely hurt by her comment.

"You want him gone then you do what you must do. I provided the opportunity."

"You mean I could have done this by myself all along?" Claire could barely believe what she was hearing.

"Only in my presence. And with my blessing," the High Priest clarified. "He is my offspring, after all."

Richard took a small step backwards, and there was fear in his eyes. "Wait just a fucking minute," he said. "You can't just stand by and let that bitch do me harm. There has to be a rule."

"I can, and I must," The High Priest offered little condolence. "I promised her, and I have my own self-preservation to think about. That's the only *rule* that applies here."

"That's not fair," Richard whined.

"You always were an obnoxious, entitled little shit, Richard," The High Priest sighed

"The least favorite of all of my creations, and pretty low down on the list of senior fecal spirits, too." He gave a wry smile. "Be thankful I'm giving you at least a fighting chance."

Richard grimaced and looked nervously at Claire. He took another step back.

Claire squinted her eyes together to gauge the distance between herself and her otherworldly husband. She was confident that she should be able to hit him with the tablets from where she was standing—she'd not been best pitcher in her middle school's baseball team two years in a row for nothing. Claire raised her arm and took aim.

In the blinking of an eye, Richard's arm shot out towards her. It elongated to treble its length to reach her, and his powerful fingers grasped her forearm. With a deft, violent twist, Richard snapped Claire's bones like kindling.

Claire's scream was deep and throaty and filled with agony and anguish. She collapsed to her knees, and the green tablets spilled from her hand as the thinner of her two arm bones stabbed through her skin, and her arm turned liquid red.

Without relinquishing the hold on his wife's arm, Richard covered the distance between them in a heartbeat and was upon her with his free hand landing ugly punches about her head, until she lay prone on the ground.

For her own part, Claire threw punches of her own, determined not to go down without a good scrap. Although she only had use of her left hand, her fist hit home, and she could feel whatever Richard had for face bones crunching beneath her knuckles and his flesh squishing as if it were already losing its realness. He rocked back with each punch, and brown goo spilled from his nose and mouth.

"Stay down, bitch," Richard growled.

Claire had no such intention and struggled against her husband's weight in an attempt to get to her feet. But with each gain she made, Richard knocked her back down and simply refused to let go of her shattered arm, which he continued to twist. As she fought against Richard, Claire could feel her baby rolling and kicking in her stomach, as if in the midst of its own battle.

Richard landed a well-aimed fist square in Claire's nose. Blood spattered from her nostrils, and its bridge twisted awkwardly to the left. Claire grunted and fell back in a daze, and her head connected with the moist ground with a most sickening *clonk.*

"I've had enough of waiting for you to drop your bastard. I can see that I'm just going to have to drag the fucker out myself," Richard snarled, as he finally let go of Claire's arm and pinned her, supine to the ground. Claire ignored the searing pain in her arm and slapped at Richard with both hands. Her doubled vision threw off her aim, and she managed only to hit the side of his head and his softening chin.

Richard yanked Claire's jeans down with one hand whilst his other fended off her flailing fists. Claire's jeans slid easily down her thighs, being of the type with a wide, elastic waistband that were designed especially for the mother-to-be. Next, he tore away her panties, and along with them a clump of unruly, dense pubic hair. He pulled a face at the sight between his wife's legs.

"I didn't realize you'd let yourself go so much, darling." Richard's clipped accent grated on Claire's nerves.

Claire struggled to sit up, but Richard pushed her down with a fat brown tendril that had sprouted from the center of his broad chest. It thumped hard between his wife's breasts and pressed her against the ground. Claire's head connected with the floor again, and she began to feel consciousness slip away from her.

"No!" she cried out her protest; this was not the way things were supposed to go! She had come all this way—put herself through this surreal horror—to be rid of the thing she'd married, not to hand him, on a plate, the very thing he wanted. She renewed her struggles, twisting her torso side to side to fight against the fecal spirit's preternatural strength.

Richard yanked Claire's legs wide apart with such ferocity that her hip joints popped. He held them open by her knees, and his penis began to fatten and grow and snake its way towards her exposed vagina. As his dick neared its target, a pair of long, curved hooks grew from its tip—all the better for ripping baby out with.

Claire twisted her head to the side, as much to

avoid witnessing the vile thing her husband was becoming as in her effort to be free of him. Her face scraped against the rough ground, and she felt something small and round dig into her cheek.

She almost cried when she saw what the thing was. It was one of the tablets she'd dropped when Richard had broken her arm. Adjacent to that green circle was another tablet and a little way past that, yet another. There were four in total, and Claire couldn't imagine when she'd last seen such a wonderful sight.

Richard's fat, slime drenched appendage nudged into Claire's vagina and stretched the delicate flesh wide open, as it invaded her body.

Claire clenched her pelvic muscles as tight as her kegal exercises had taught her in order to hinder the dick's progress enough to buy her a second or two of time. She then twisted her torso and strained her neck to roll her mouth over the tablet, which she sucked up into her mouth. Along with it came the foul-tasting grit that coated the sewer's ground. Claire strained a little more and bagged the second tablet, and by the third and fourth, she had become quite the expert.

"There's no use trying to escape, my love," Richard sneered. "You might as well lay back and enjoy this." He thrust his hips, and his pliant penis slid deep inside Claire and probed at her cervix. He watched with fascination as his wife's swollen abdomen churned and bulged—it was as if the child within knew what horrendous fate was fast approaching.

Claire summoned strength from reserves she didn't know she had. She slammed her good arm against the thick tendril that had her pinned down and knocked it aside. Quickly, she sat herself up using her broken arm, despite the white-hot spear of agony that shot all the way up to her shoulder. Looking directly into Richard's surprised, smug eyes, Claire spat the chewed-up mess of green tablets and thick saliva from her mouth and into his face.

"Dirty bitch!" Richard yelled at her; his tone indignant. He looked across at the High Priest who looked on with benign indifference at the melee from his place by the altar. Richard's expression was very much a childish *did you see what she just did?!* He looked like a little kid who just had his bike stolen. Richard bared his teeth at Claire and pushed his dick harder inside her. At the same time, he made its girth increase to incredibly uncomfortable proportions. He wiped his face with the back of his hand to remove the disgusting green mess that clung there. "I'm going to make you bloody well pay for that…"

Richard's nose crumbled away against his knuckles, along with his upper lip, which drooled down his chest like melting chocolate. "Wha-?" he exclaimed, as he explored the hole on the center of his once-handsome face. As he spoke, a torrent of teeth pitter-patted from his mouth and clattered noisily on the hard ground beside Claire.

Claire wrenched her knees from her husband's grasp and kicked him away.

He landed flat on his backside and the jolt dislodged his jawbone, and it slid without ceremony down his chest and fell on to his lap. Richard's fat prick slurped out of her vagina and flopped on the floor between the two of them, like a freshly landed deep-sea fish.

"Payback, asshole." Claire just couldn't resist.

Hands grasping with desperation at his decaying face, which slid and fell apart in fat, waxy gobbets, Richard let out an ear-splitting ululation that filled the atrium with a siren song of agony and injustice, as his tongue flapped loosely in the gaping maw that was once his perfect mouth. He scrabbled to his feet, leaving several fingers on the ground in the process, and staggered away from Claire, his melting dick lolling limply between his thighs.

Richard's dissolution went far quicker than Claire imagined it would. His screams rapidly became little more than thick, clogged gurgles as his head collapsed in on itself, and the brown goop of his brain degenerated into a lumpy, viscous mess, much in the same fashion as the Bela Lugosi vampires of yesteryear. His hands—where he had attempted to wipe away the masticated Imodium from his face—shed their flesh in desiccating clumps and shreds to expose the crumbling bones beneath. Before long, little more remained of the digits than stubs of tan-colored, collapsing bone.

Headless and mercifully silent, Richard dropped to his knees. The decay that had begun in his face had spread around his body like a wildfire, and the unholy stink of Indian food and sour tequila effused from his rank approximation of flesh. Richard's skin blistered and popped and dissolved away, and when it could no longer hold in his internal organs, they slopped out onto the sewer floor to return to their constituent brown slime. Richard's dissolving corpse crumpled, and what little remained collapsed to the ground, where it undulated and shifted as it broke apart.

In the end, all that remained of the ethereal creature that had been Richard Richards was a shrinking pool of lumpy brown, rank-smelling crap. Throw in the expensive silk panties and paper feminine hygiene bag with the picture of the stern-faced Victorian lady, and Claire's husband would have been back precisely where he'd started.

Claire watched with repulsed fascination and horror at the mess, and the thought crossed her mind that perhaps the process would have to totally run in reverse to be complete.

But, lucky for her, it didn't.

"It never ceases to amaze," the High Priest broke the eerie silence as Richard's disassembled body soaked into the greasy floor, "that given our eons of evolution, we can be so easily defeated by a common stool hardener." He gave what was almost a smile, as he watched the end of his offspring's demise.

Claire scrabbled around to pick up the remaining tablets and then got to her feet. Without taking the time to pull up her pants, Claire rounded on the High Priest—the one whose sweet seduction had gotten her involved in this sick nightmare in the first place.

"It's your turn now, *shithead*." She raised her good arm and took aim.

The High Priest shook his head and smiled quite serenely. "I think you should quit while you're ahead, my dear," he said. "You have what you came for, now I strongly suggest that you leave." He glanced over at his pale, glistening followers who surrounded the detective. The guy holding Howgard's confiscated gun did so directly at her face. "While you still can, that is."

To underline his point, from somewhere deep in the darkest, most foul reaches of the New Orleans sewer there came a reverberating growl that comprised a legion of hellish voices. Claire's body shivered involuntarily, and a brutal chill settled in her marrow that made her feel so utterly terrified.

She lowered her arm.

"You may want to take that with you." The High Priest looked down at the altar, at the baby that slumbered between its dead mother's sagging breasts. Between the mother's flaccid, blood drenched legs lay the slack, jellied clod of the placenta, its severed cord dangling over the edge of the infernal altar.

"You disgusting cun-" Claire's rage bubbled over, and she raised her arm once more and murderous intent blazed in her eyes.

A monumental pain hit Claire like a donkey-kick to the guts. She yowled out her agony, and a torrent of hot fluids gushed from her vagina and splashed steaming to the floor. Claire felt her legs giving out beneath her, and she grasped the rough edge of the altar to steady herself. Another contraction hit her hard, and she could do nothing but watch the last of her green tablets as they bounced away from her drenched feet.

Claire grunted and clutched at her belly to prevent her child from bursting out through its distended walls. Another wave of pain coursed through Claire, and her knees finally betrayed her and deposited her back on the ground. Through the haze of panic and pain, Claire could see the detective making her way over. The pallid collective surrounding her had parted enough to allow her through, although that gun was still trained on the back of her skull as she made her way over.

"Goodbye, Claire." The High Priest loomed over her prone body. "It has been a pleasure to see you again." And Claire remembered his body with its rich, earthy scent sweating and pressed tight against hers, his magnificent cock crammed into her willing ass and the overwhelming *fullness* sensation that he'd given her. The High Priest took a step forward and reached for her.

Then, all went very black indeed for Claire Jepson.

EPILOGUE

One of the babies needed changing again, Claire could smell it. The stink hung thick and acrid in the sterile air, even managing to overpower the hospital's institutional aroma of antiseptic, blood and sweat.

She crawled with a great reluctance out of her bed. As she did so, she barked her shin on the chilly metal frame and cursed beneath her breath. The stitches below her once round belly pulled on her slit flesh as she straightened herself up - they'd had to cut her infant daughter out of her body in the end.

Claire didn't remember too much about how she got to the hospital, or how come she seemed to have ended up with two babies instead of just the one. She figured that the extra one—a boy if the blue blankets and bonnet were anything to go by—was the one she'd seen slopping out of the poor woman on the altar down in the dark, dank sewers that haunted her dreams.

Claire also guessed that the detective had something to do with her escape from that nightmarish place, too; she could see her hanging around in the hallway outside the private room, talking to one of the nurses. Occasionally, the detective would cast a glance Claire's way, as if she were genuinely concerned about her welfare.

Claire lifted her daughter gently out of the plastic hospital crib. She placed the baby gently onto the changing table and undid the onesie poppers that snuggled between her tiny, chubby thighs. The baby—two days old, and Claire hadn't been inspired enough to name her yet—looked up at her mom with wide, blue eyes and made that faint, mewling sound that only newborns and kittens seem to be able to make.

"Okay, stinky-ass," Claire cooed as she lifted up the baby's rear end. Claire undid the diaper and slipped it away. The diaper was nasty, all clotted up with the thick tar-like meconium that babies expel shortly after birth (some even during, the thought of which filled Claire with abject horror; the thought of that disgusting stuff inside her was revolting, even after everything she'd been through) and was the remnants of the fetal gut lining and a whole manner of other repulsive substances.

"Jeez, that stinks." Claire wrinkled her nose as she scraped diligently at the sticky mess on her daughter's butt cheeks with unscented baby wipes.

"So would you if you'd been stuck up a baby's ass for nine months," the mess in the diaper retorted, and Claire thought this time its accent sounded somewhat Australian.

THE END

ABOUT THE AUTHOR

James H. longmore hails originally from Doncaster, a mining town in the south of Yorkshire, Northern England; he relocated with his family to Houston, Texas in 2010. James boasts an honors degree in Zoology and a former career background in sales, marketing, and business. He is an accomplished, published author (and publisher), and ghostwriter of popular fiction - he writes across a wide range of genres and subjects: novels, shorts, and screenplays. He has written and directed award-winning short movies, is an affiliate member of the Horror Writer's Association, and has run/hosted the popular podcast/radio show *The New Panic Room* since early 2016,
In addition, James is the founder and owner of the indie publisher, *HellBound Books Publishing LLC* (est. 2016), which publishes horror, bizarro, and a whole manner of dark fiction.

http://www.panicroomradio.com

http://www.hellboundbookspublishing.com/authorpage_longmore.html

James H Longmore

ALSO BY JAMES H LONGMORE

BUDS

Wildus Guidry, amateur scientist extraordinaire, invents time travel. To his bitter disappointment, he discovers his device only transports him mere fractions of a second into the past. Inhabiting the new, alternate world of that fractional past is a variation of *Homo sapiens* that reproduce asexually by budding and uses sex as a recreational pastime and as a means of feeding. Disappointed by his discovery, Guidry and his entrepreneurial girlfriend decide to bring back some of the Buds and open the world's most bizarre and exclusive brothel - the Buds' unique appearance as grotesquely erotic conjoined twins, triplets, quadruplets (and more!) prove to be incredibly popular amongst the brothel's elite clientele. Of course, all goes terribly wrong as the Buds turn out to be not as benign as first thought, and chaos and the end of the world ensues.

Buds is a unique, sexy take on the popular time travel trope, and a must for all lovers of conjoined twin tales. An erotic, at times brutal and disturbing, story told with lashings of dark humor.

TENEBRION

"The Devil's in the detail."

Amateur filmmakers inadvertently invoke a demon when they break into an abandoned school to perform and film an authentic Black Mass for their entry into a short movie competition.

Dave Priestley and his crew film in Watsonville elementary school – the site of a horrific tragedy nine years before.

Tenebrion – the malevolent demon of darkness – makes preparations of its own within the dark recesses of Hell. The demon requires a specific set of circumstances and sacrifices to rend a fissure between the worlds and set free its brethren; it has manipulated humans for centuries to put things into place, and the moviemakers are the unfortunate, final pieces of its nefarious puzzle.

Priestley, ever the stickler for authenticity and detail, accidentally sets free the denizen of Hell. And while Priestley and his skeptical friends attempt to return Tenebrion to the pit of Hades, it hunts them all down – one by one – for inclusion in its hellish gateway.

THE EROTIC ODYSSEY OF COLTON FORSHAY

Colton Forshay dreams himself into a bizarre sexual dystopia - a world in which nothing is as it should be, it alternately rains semen and menstrual blood, sickening sex acts and sexual violence are the norm, and the currency is deviant sexual acts.
In this dream world, Colton inexplicably finds he has gotten his dog pregnant and his wife is brutally murdered as a contestant on a popular TV show.
At first disturbed, then intrigued - and shamefully aroused - by his dreams of the other world, Colton is drawn in deeper and begins to spend more time there with the help of sleeping pills. His real-world wife forces Colton to see a psychiatrist, who encourages him to explore the dream world. And thus, our hero embarks on an odyssey with his dog/son, Eric, to discover the disturbing truth behind his dream world.

There, Colton gets caught up with the resistance, who believe the government - lead by a mysterious, telepathic ocelot - controls the people by means of dreams of another realm, which sounds uncannily like his actual world.
The storyline alternates between Colton's real and fantasy dream worlds, and the two become inexorably blurred until Colton unearths a disturbing truth not entirely against the perverse tastes he's developed.
This is fantastical tale populated by a whole host of bizarre characters, set in an incredibly peculiar world. Chock-full of startling, sexy imagery and told with incredibly dark humor, Colton Forshay is a bizarro tale both engaging and disturbing.

PEDE:

An affectionate homage to the creature feature! The once luxurious Mountainview Spa Hotel in the heart of California's Coachella valley lies decaying, abandoned and heavily boarded up - the site of a radioactive, "dirty" bomb explosion five years' previously. Zoology Professor, Jane Lucas, harbors a lifelong phobia of *Scolopendra gigantea,* the Giant Centipede, despite being the world's leading authority on the creature. Following the savage deaths of two teenagers who broke into the hotel to cavort in the natural underground spa and the discovery of centipede remains almost three times natural size, the professor teams up with four of her students to investigate.
Their expedition soon becomes a fight for survival when they're trapped inside the hotel with a gang of violent thugs and a voracious swarm of oversized centipedes that infest the place - and then discover another creature even more terrifying is hunting in the Mountainview's deserted hallways: a centipede of impossibly monstrous proportions… ravenous and desperate to feed.

FLANAGAN

"The Devil's Rejects meets Fifty Shades – heart-pounding, gut-wrenching, sexy as all hell, and with a twist you'll never see coming!"

Meet the Sewells, an all-American couple; happily married for ten years, respected high school teachers, still crazy about one another, and with a mutually-shared dark side.

During their annual Spring Break vacation to recharge batteries and reconnect, the Sewells are waylaid by a perverse gang of misfits in the one-horse, North Texas town of Flanagan.

Taken hostage to be the focus of the gang's twisted games, the Sewells are brutalized into performing vicious physical, sexual, and emotional acts upon one another, until events take an unexpected turn, triggered by an unintentional death.

As their circumstances descend into the worse nightmare imaginable, the Sewells find themselves involved in an altogether different situation...

BLOOD AND KISSES

"Think of what late greats James Herbert and Richard Laymon may have given birth to had they ever collaborated" - Richard Chizmar

The definitive short story collection from James H Longmore - an eclectic mix of dark horror, bizarro and *Twilight Zone* style tales of the downright disturbing. Welcome to the long-awaited collection from the writer of horror novels *'Pede* and *Tenebrion*; a foreword by Richard Chizmar (co-author of *Gwendy's Button Box* with Stephen King), 18 short stories, 5 flash fiction, and a poem - all skin-crawling, soul-shredding tales of the darkest things that skulk among the night's inky shadows and of the everyday gone horribly awry.

Discover the implication of technology becoming self-aware, enjoy the acquaintance of a charismatic new pastor promising his flock a brand new place to worship his God, spend a little time in the company of a nice young man who is inexorably caught up in his home town's terrible secret. Then, there's Cupid's revelation he's never experienced love, we discover that very emotion alive and not so well among the ruins of a post-zombie apocalyptic world, and bear witness to childhood innocence forever destroyed in a distant, war-torn city.

Observe, too any unsavory individual's obsession with the ever-elusive snuff movie, and join an elderly bunch of forgetful sleuths out to solve the mystery of brutal deaths that occur with alarming regularity at their memory care facility.

Now, have you ever considered what may happen should you have the misfortune to bump into your family's doppelgangers on a long, tedious road trip? And, can you even begin to imagine being the doting father who finally realizes the apple of his eye's true identity, or the parents who spend what is left of their crumbling lives waiting by a silent telephone for news of their addict son?

There is more, Dear Reader, much, much more; for within the pages we have devils, demons and ghosts, lycanthropes, and demi-gods, all rubbing nefarious shoulders with the most vile of Hell's offspring, who have slithered up from the netherworld to doff their caps and wish us all the sweetest of dreams…

FEEDER

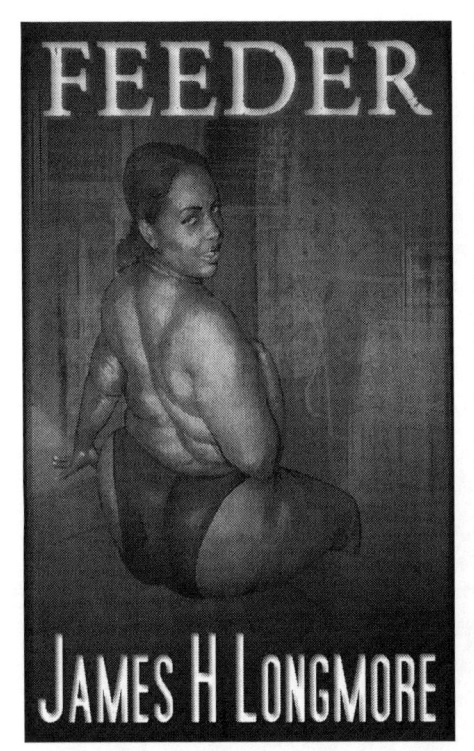

A deliciously bizarro, darkly disturbing peek into the world of gainers and feeders: grotesquely obese individuals and those people who facilitate their growth for the lascivious pleasure of both parties.
The heroine of the piece, Novella, Embarks upon a journey into the dreadful netherworld that dwells within the obese, fleshy folds of a woman especially engorged for the perverted delights of her Internet audience. Aided and abetted by a former feeder, she fights to escape before the grim portal closes and she's trapped forever in the ghastly realm of fat, flesh, and death most gruesome.

I AM JOE'S UNWANTED PENIS

A darkly comedic tribute to the much-loved Reader's Digest series *'I am Joe's...(insert body part here)'* and a bizarre parody of the Bruce Jenner story, *I Am Joe's Unwanted Penis* is told from the point of view of a penis discarded as a man is surgically transformed into a woman.

Upon learning if his high-profile previous owner's regret at having made the transformation, the penis embarks upon a perilous journey for them to be reunited - aided and abetted by a motley, wonderfully personable, and engaging selection of other discarded body parts.

In parts grotesque, laugh-out-loud funny, and undeniably poignant, in others, *I Am Joe's Unwanted Penis* is a buddy-story absolutely like no other!

**A HellBound Books LLC
Publication 2021**

www.hellboundbookspublishing.com

Printed in the United States of America

Made in the USA
Middletown, DE
13 August 2024